A LOT OF BULL

Tales from the Back Acres of Union Township
Marshall County, Indiana

By James F. Walsh

Contents

A LOT OF
BULL

A LOT OF BULL

Nary a man, woman or child don't think a three mile walk out on a Union Township road isn't good for fitness! Ain't that true? This here story's all about such a little walk one late winter morning. You see, Grandpa has this need to get in shape every fifty years, and seeing as how he were seventeen years past schedule, he and his big old body got up early of a cold day to walk off a half dozen donuts. (Walking a hundred yards is equal to burning off the calories from a donut, right? Grandma said so, never mind them medical experts at the walk-in, not walk-out Medical Clinic said it ain't.)

Whoever was right, (Grandma, of course), old Grandpa was lugging his suitcases (ain't no need to say they were attached fore and aft) on the State Road when he heard cattle bellowing. He didn't see no animal, being as it wasn't sun-up. (Sun-up in Hoosier land is a single beam through a billow between thick clouds opened by a strong wind). Them bawling cattle sounded like nothing city folks ever heard. If it can be described, it sounded most like a teen-ager's self-sorry moaning after a grounding. Anyhow, Grandpa figured some of those critters must have unlatched farmer Hezekiah's pasture gate to cross the road to farmer Noah's corn crib. Weren't of no mind to Grandpa seeing as how Noah wasn't popular with his own herd, holding out on feeding them choice kemels, as he held out for more pennies a bushel than the co-op settled on the other grain farmers. It figgered some little doggies would get at Noah's gourmet corn.

Now, Grandpa walked down the hilly State Road right easy enough, he was real good at obeying gravity, but on the way up was puffing like them whales that blow off steam out there in deep water. Then, out of his good left eye, the right looked east instead of north, up on the hill, he spied something round as a five hundred gallon water tank. To his fading memory, there weren't no water tank up there on that hill, least wise one that moved, snorted and had a huge tuning fork up on top. (Tuning forks are them funny hooked things that the little sissy fellow brings with him when he tunes Grandma's piano, as if she can tell the difference.) Seeing that the water tank hopped, skipped and jumped, right then and there, Grandpa settled on going to one of them fancy eye-doctors in Culver town now that Medicare was like to foot some of the big bill. Pushing it out of his mind, the little of it left under even less hair, Grandpa struggled farther up that dog-gone hill when that water tank took it on itself to grow bigger and paw ground. Dogged if the ground it plowed didn't tremble. That good eye blinked. What on earth was happening to his five senses? Well four; maybe three; then again two. After Grandma's last batch of boiled potatoes smothered in garlic and hot pepper gravy, the sense of smell and taste were still on the road to recovery. Grandpa never did hear good, especially back in elementary school when he weren't taking a nap.

What was with the water tank? It took to coming

down the hill, changing size to a jeep. Not an Army jeep, mind, but one of them vehicles Union Town-shippers latched horns on when they go out funning Culver folks on the big roads. (Come to think on it, there ain't no big roads in Union Township, just back roads.) Didn't that Jeep rumble farther downhill, growing to the size of a Cadillac, then stretching into a Suburban Utility Vehicle, next sprouting larger than a RV, expanding into a dump truck until looming larger than a garbage truck. Grandpa wondered was he a waste product to be lifted into a bin? He said 'oh my' more often than he said it after a first look at each of the five new babies Grandma brought home in the old army duffel bag. He was 'oh mying' because of what was coming down on him. It weren't no garbage truck! Danged if it wasn't a bull, not one of them Ferdinands you hear folks tell of, mind, but a snorting, thundering, big horned creature up to making a pie out of the pumpkin on the State Road. (Grandpa's overhang of hair still had a touch of red). He saw right off the critter was fit to be tied, and had he any rope and someone stupid enough to do up the four footed snorter, there would have been a 'thank ye' soon as the stowed-up fellow got off the critical list. This here critter was bellowing louder than children after a bath. (Once a week wasn't too much, except, who could tell which of his five was which after a scrubbing?)

That charging critter was as long as Grandma's piano, tail whipping back and forth black and big as a crowbar. Not Grandma's, the bull's! Was the critter's scowl from no breakfast? Grandpa weren't no bale of hay, no matter he was as round. A woe-is-me thought crossed his mind seeing the horns of the bull not so far up the hill and Grandpa not so far down the hill as everybody thought. Yet, he gave a recollect as to how he never got around to telling neighbor Noah, the farmer, his super corn wasn't from good farming methods but from Grandpa's leaky septic tank drain field.

     Living in the country takes old fashion know how. Grandpa quick saw, just off to his right on Noah's lawn, a mole tunnel with ridges so high they looked foothills to the Rocky Mountains. (Moles is appreciated out in the country for cheap aeration of lawns clear of old combines, tractors and pickups. The bigger moles are hired out to do dumps. Handy animals, them moles.) Back to Grandpa. That was all of him that bull viewed, the back. Grandpa done run up the mole ridge so fast only elbows, heels and his hinder acre was visible to them pursuing red eyes. Grandpa took to hiding behind one side of a tree, the bull, horns the sizes of giant cacti, the other side. Grandpa would have picked a tree with a trunk circular as a water tower, not a willow too small to weep, if he weren't rather misty eyed himself. When the critter took to faking to the right of the sliver of wood while stabbing mean horns to the left, old Grandpa's boxing instincts done rose up like his breakfast was ready to do. He faked a jab of his own, a cross, another jab. Now anyone watching the match between that there bull and the over-the-hill boxer, the two about even on the weigh-in scale, would have yelled 'the fight's fixed' so long did they dance around that weeping willow! Grandpa's feet were so nimble, his prancing around would have shamed a fancy Spanish Toreador! That there frustrated bull didn't so much as land a horn. Grandpa done wore down the ton of meat. (The critter weighed the ton!) Bored it didn't get in a boring, it ambled off hunting better odds and something not so big.

Humble as he is, Grandpa doesn't want this story to take on heroic dimensions among his grandchildren, them who can read. Who can't, Grandpa will tell it again.

Now, there's a little twist to this here story. Grandpa found it out when he went over to give the piece of his mind yet remaining to farmer Hezekiah right in front of Homer, the hired man and Homer's faithful follower, Hired Dog. The straight of it is, it weren't no bull at all coming down the State Road like a box car, but a heifer! Hezekiah and Hired Man took to funning right mean about the difference! Now, in fairness to Grandpa, he weren't about to take time out to give one of them gender test to the rampaging critter the working end of horns, and like the friendly galoot he is, he took the funning good natured. But that danged Hired Dog showing up over to Grandpa's place the days since and snickering, plagues Grandpa's even temper.

RINGING HOGS OUT TO UNION TOWNSHIP

Back in the city where Grandpa chawed down on fried carp, he never gave a hoot about who brung the bewiskered fish in from Asia to gobble up river weeds. All he knew was them bottom greens had plenty of vitamins and minerals because the carp grew big as alligators in the old Missouri! Took three men to wrestle one out of the water to solid ground and fresh hands to do it in. Grandpa got his carp fillets icy-fresh off the fish monger's horse drawn wagon. Tasty as could be in sandwiches, sure enough, grilled as they was over charcoal. Still, a man had to be careful grit didn't sand down the last of his usable teeth.

Grandpa figured on leaving carp fillets behind in favor of meat cuts when he bought the place out to south Union township. He done bought out there on the advice of a big-city real estate agent who said land sold cheap way out in the country. Especially if it were land beyond Culver's zoning, for in town, politicians tossed around massive assessments heavier than what fat cattle dropped out in the pastures.

Settling down where fences were corn rows and chowing down on fresh cuts, even at his Church's hog roast over a fire of bounced checks, (fire chief wasn't able to explain why the bounced checks of church going folks burned hotter than the fire in the place they was likely heading), Grandpa didn't give a think to the pedigree of the tonnage of meat flopped on his plate. And for sure didn't the old carnivore lash himself to the table until the bones shined after Grandma took a pan full of pork chops off the grill and he ate for the billions of poor folks in China like he was taught during the great depression? It never crossed his wit's dregs to ponder where all them savory cuts got their starts. The sum of it was Grandpa never heard no talk on live hogs.

You're wondering what's the hooting on about live hogs? Well, let me get to the telling.

On a windy day, a nor-westerner flogging his place, Grandpa caught whiff of air mindful of a carp too long out of the Tippecanoe River. Being the one sense still unlocked, he followed his pug nose and caught sight of Hezekiah's hogs rounder and smellier than land locked river fish! The porkers were rounder and smellier, not Hezekiah, though he was a close second. They was snorting and snuffling in a pen. Hezekiah too! Grandpa finally realized where the pork he'd inhaled was farrowed.

What could he do about live hogs as neighbors? A man had about all he could handle with Hezekiah, Noah, hired man and hired dog. Them and hogs too? Hard choice! It called for thought. Just where Grandpa could call to find a thought he couldn't figure, excepting he gave birth to one on his own. He scratched the leather old Indian chief Running Board called scalp. Sparks flew. Grandpa strained his eyes and flapped ears. He had a think! (Never made it to a full-fledged thought.) He'd go up to the County Seat and find a wise old lawyer.

Forgetting 'wise' and settling on 'old', Grandpa sat the other side of the cash register. Lawyer Rubric, ('I bill big, therefore, I am') was just reinstated again so collected his fee up-front. He gave this legal opinion: "Grandpa moved to the nuisance. Live hogs, Hezekiah, Noah, hired man and hired dog had longevity. Any city slicker who bought in agricultural country had no right complaining on farming hogs. That was the law of it."

Grandpa took to the opinion like it was the Chicago Cubs scoring the World Series winning run in the bottom of the ninth, pure fiction! Still, knowing how to read comic books, he'd not take up reading yarns at this stage, afraid he'd miss the coach to Heaven. He settled down to living with nor-westerner's fragrance of Hezekiah's hogs.

Early of a morning, walking stick in hand, Grandpa hustled his working apparatus, (him and it were draped with a reflector vest for speeding pickups to better target). He climbed state road hill when, wouldn't you know up alongside pulled a pickup with farmer Hezekiah looped over the steering wheel and hired dog riding a hay bale back in the bed. Dang if hired dog didn't once again take to snickering at the sight of the slicker chased by the heifer around Noah's trees. Grandpa pretended no mind to hired dog, but the sniveling of the chortling critter could of put a Bud Abbot-Lou Costello audience to shame.

Didn't Hezekiah say, "com' on up to the pen for a ringing of the hogs, you ain't doing nothing. Got me Noah and hired man. One more hand right about do it."

Grandpa kept on a cheerful face no matter the insult on him doing nothing, but he was a man of his own, on his own, doing his own, and he would have gone his own way if hired dog hadn't repeatedly snorted disgust at the ex-city feller.

Riled and glaring back at hired dog, Grandpa said, "I'll walk right over, Hezekiah."

The pickup fogged the road up to Hezekiah's and Grandpa got on to thinking about ringing hogs. What were that all about? A circus ring full of performing hams? The Dancing Slabs of Bacons? Pig feet jitter-bugging? Pig Capades? A comedy of boars? Romeo and Piglet? The Johnny Berkshire Late Night Show? Rump and Chop Comedy Hour? Jowls' Grill? It was coming on a good time, alright, Grandpa reckoned, this ringing of the hogs.

There was a spring in his step walking the long graveled road back to where Hezekiah's boars gushed their bouquet. Strange? It weren't a three ring circus at all! Hired dog was backed away off, the look on its ugly face more frightened than Grandma's on Halloween when little ghosts came calling 'trick or treat'. It were three old boars flipped on their backs, legs tied with cord like during a chittlings robbery. Hired man's and Noah's knees were planted on one boar's belly, except they ain't had on no masks like city crooks wore. They was mightily straining to hold that huge snorter to place. Hezekiah weren't doing nothing to run off the criminals. He were accomplicing! With a knife in hand, he cut. Not appeased with legs tied with cord, Hezekiah went and tied that boar where there were nothing left after the cutting. Danged if hired man, Noah and Hezekiah didn't repeat the assault and battery with intent to maim on the other two slobbers! Hired dog was horrified. Under a hay stack, paws over eyes, snout sniveling, chin vibrating, he whined the whine of a consolidated (the school, not the student) high schooler in detention.

"What's going on, Hezekiah?" Grandpa said.

"Them boars ain't suitable for breeding no more."

"That right? Suitable don't make no difference to men up to Culver town."

"They's city folk," Hezekiah said. "Com' on Grandpa, got ringing to do. Take the top of the chute. When hired man and Noah run a hog down the chute, the critter going to try to leap head first out this here end. He don't if'en you slam this here cut four by four a'gin his neck and pin him good and tight a'gin the other four by four. You hold on, I ring. Rings in the snout keep the hogs from rooting. When ringings done, you let go the hog."

Grandpa sized up slamming the heavy wooden handle on the hog's neck as it leapt to clear the hurdle of the chute. No pain! This was farming a seasoned city boy like him could do. He'd hit 350 his last baseball season with a bat about as big as the four by four. The first hog came running and vaulted like a pigskin kicked over the goal post for a double overtime victory! Grandpa slammed the handle. He pinned the massive neck against the other side. Eyes popped, ears laid back, snout whipped. Not Grandpa's, the hog's! What a snorting! Grandpa's! He fought with everything left in him, not much, to keep that handle pressed against the agitated two hundred pounds of dynamite. There was more dusk kicked up in that chute than a GI tank did in Desert Storm when Hezekiah clipped rings into the snout as if a store clerk putting staples through a grocery bag. No sooner told to let the hog clear the chute than another hog bigger than a professional football fullback hurdled up. Down went the handle; up went the snorting; in went the rings; up went the dust! Again and again until forty hogs were rung. Finally, when Noah and hired man came out the chute, and hired dog out from under the hay stack, Grandpa let loose the handle. He was all rung out!

"Good day's work, Grandpa," Hezekiah said.

"Make a farmer of you yet," Noah said.

"Did right good," hired man said, hired dog now at his side, head bobbing.

"Thanks men, hired dog. Must admit I never saw so much fussing and fuming. The way those hogs tossed their snouts at me, you'd think they had teeth to take a chunk. Can you imagine?"

They couldn't imagine the slicker was so dumb. Hired dog kicked off the hilarity, snickering like as to bust a pumpkin gut. Hezekiah's belly flopped like molasses poured on pancakes. Noah took to snorting until tears primed the pump. Hired man giggled loud enough to embarrass a gaggle of eight grade girls talking about ninth grade boys.

What was they laughing on? Grandpa looked around. The moment he saw teeth in the mouths of the rung hogs, he knew a funning on him for not knowing the huge size of hog molars would be repeated all over the township. Hezekiah, Noah and hired man was mostly human, so they had the right of funning another human.

Not hired dog. Grandpa weren't of a mind to again long suffer its jollity over him. He took in hand a length of boar cord. A baleful eye fell on hired dog as the cord whistled turning in the air. Hired dog weren't no idiot mongrel. He reckoned Grandpa's purpose with the boar cord and hustled back to the hay stack to burrow deeply enough to embarrass a team of moles drilling through permafrost.

Nowadays, Grandpa won't go walking no more without a length of boar cord whistling in the ozone!

UNION TOWNSHIP'S PECULIAR LAW

Grandpa never figured a particularly peculiar law stretched its meaning to cover his *bleep* (the part of the anatomy that followed the rest of him) when walking the remote roads of Union Township. He was ticketed under that peculiar law however, and was summoned by Deputy Duty to the Justice of the Peace Court.

Let me get on to telling how Grandpa got hit with Deputy Duty's ticket.

Grandpa was a law abider as law abider's go, (not counting putting Fast Food's plastic spoon and cup in the trash over to the church's garbage can before services). Darned if on one foggy morning when Grandpa was out on the road parting the mist into halves, the Deputy, waiving a ticket book out of his pickup's window, didn't pull up beside the ambulating old timer and direct him off the side white line to the shoulder.

Wasn't much of a shoulder; more a cliff. Grandpa stepped, missed his footing and fell, rolling down the sharp slope like a cut log. He tumbled through Noah's little woods squashing budding timber. Hard as it was to believe, Grandpa cut a new road right through the little woods. Now Noah hadn't a need for a new road right there, the long tarmac one doing him proud. Still, Noah would have appreciated the low cost of the fleshy steamroller, Grandpa huffing hot air every turn of his body, mind over toes. Fortunately, (or unfortunately), there was a deep ditch at the bottom of the knoll or no telling how far he might have rolled. At the sight of the hulk flopping stomach over back, cattle the other side of the ditch got jumpy, moaning like a corralled herd heading up a ramp to the slaughter house. Suddenly, Grandpa disappeared from sight, a tall water spout marking the precise location where his belly (and the rest in tow) flopped. The dairy herd butted heads to win the closest spot to gaze at the wonder in the water.

Deputy Duty, thinking the ancient geezer was fleeing the long arm of the law, pulled his pickup over to road side. No prehistoric Neanderthal was going to light out on him. Duty came out of the pickup screaming and yelling, hightailing down the newly cut road, legs whirling like windmills, pencil in one hand, ticket book in the other, pages flapping in the breeze.

Meanwhile, Grandpa, aching in every joint, struggled up the embankment like a turtle who'd lost his shell. Seeing a mountain of flesh hurling at him, Grandpa ducked, worried he'd be pushed fossil deep back into the ditch's muck by one of the township's finest, but momentum carried Duty like a gymnast approaching a pommel horse. He jumped, missed his distance and slammed into the ditch's other dirt wall, torso, arms, legs and chest badge making deep impressions. He slithered down the muddy bank like a boneless snake and oozed like a frog into deep runoff water, its head source percolating out of the cattle pasture. Thinking of those critters, the sight of the lawman broad jumping was fright enough to panic them to a stampede. For sure, Noah wasn't going to get sweet milk the day's second milking.

Grandpa let loose of the scraw in hand and slipped back down. He grabbed the floundering fish by his shirt and pulled the groggy lawman out of the deep to the grassy bank, but hadn't strength in his hurt bones to tow unconscious bulk the whole distance up. Not after road blazing, swimming laps in cattle runoff and climbing the embankment. Quick to think, Grandpa crawled up the slope again and hurried up hill to fetch the Deputy's pickup, driving down the new cut road to wench the soaked man up from sludge. Grandpa wiggled the hook on the end of the wire until it caught Duty's gun belt, then returned to the pickup and reversed gears. Duty came up out of the mire like a hooked alligator. (Come to think about it, Grandpa said Duty looked more a crocodile than alligator.)

Now wouldn't you think the Deputy would appreciate the tow from deep in cattle runoff to dry terra firma? Not Duty! Mad as a crocodile when he came to, he motioned for Grandpa to get out of the pickup, then warned the old hyena to keep quiet on Duty's missing his jump across the ditch and stampeding Noah's cows or the law would come down with a second charge of 'fleeing an officer in the performance of his duty'.

"Second charge?" Grandpa said. He wasn't a total dimwit. "What's the first charge?"

Deputy Duty was clear on it. "Old man, you got to hang a red reflective triangle on the back of a wide load on a foggy day. Coming up on you on the road, I didn't see no triangle."

"What wide load? Red reflective triangle? What

you talking, Deputy? I wasn't driving."

Duty said, "I know old timer. Still, all I could see from the pickup was one very wide-e-e-e rump. Law calls for a triangle. No triangle, I ticket!"

Speechless for once, Grandpa stood still as a silo while Duty whittled a new point on his pencil to write the ticket. Having written, he handed it over, ditch mud and all. "Appear at the Township Justice of the Peace Court tomorrow." Nothing more of interest, certainly not the astonishment on the face of the offender who had the goods on him, (he missed his jump and scared the cows), Duty hopped in and wheeled his pickup up Noah's new cut to the paved road and drove away.

Grandpa couldn't believe he'd been ticketed for a wide load and summoned to appear at JP Court! He took a gander at the small print on the back of the ticket. Squinting, he read the township's law: *Except as provided in subsection (b) hereof, but absolutely excluded in subsections (c), (d), (e), or (f) as modified by the Township, wide-load shall mean any vehicle or other mode of transportation that carries a load, cargo or other thing which displaces more of the road than the distance between the edge of a lane on a two way road to the center line, whether or not a white line marks the said edge, or a yellow line (dotted or continual) marks the center of said road. In all such situations, the mode of transportation shall tail a red reflective triangle or similar warning to other trailing modes of transportation.*

Eyes owl wide, Grandpa reasoned subsection (b) of

the law was clear as fog. His *bleep* was a wide load under subsection (b)? He read more. Excluded altogether from township roads were *Subsection (c) box cars, (d) biplanes, (e) armored tanks and (f) ocean sailing ships.* Grandpa wondered when last a Monon boxcar, Wright Brothers' biplane, Patton tank or a Chinese Junk rolled down a township road? Another twist to the ticket mollified Grandpa's hurt feelings. His *bleep* wasn't in the same category as those excluded wide loads. Still, Duty's ticket implied it was of a magnitude sufficient that it necessitated a dangling red lighted lantern or similar warning. Grandpa pondered on it. Sure enough, there was a time his *bleep* might have been excluded in subsection (g) if he'd lived in the township years back when in the boxing ring his seconds said there was no need to turn the other cheek and provided him with two corner stools between rounds.

Grandpa had his *bleep* many a year with no prior tickets on it, particularly since he'd come to the township and exercised a hundredweight off its bones. The man's amplitude wasn't what it once was. (On glancing at it, hanging a red reflective triangle on the remnants while walking on back roads could have been wise.)

Anyway, Grandpa wasn't one to enter a plea of guilty. He knew the burden of proof was on Duty to win his case against the accused. Besides, pleading guilty led to a paying a fine on what nature created with zoom lenses. That was contra to Grandpa's not so meek disposition. He'd try his own case. If he lost, he hoped as a choice to a fine, the word **otherwise** written in forbidding bold print on the ticket meant community service picking up road side beer cans left by the shallow brained who messed up their own steadiness while contributing to the riches of sober beer barons.

Where was the JP court anyway? Lo and behold! The address was the same as Hezekiah's farm just down the road from Grandpa's place. He figured, rather than build a JP Courtroom, country tax paying folks saved tax dollars renting from Hezekiah. Was he JP? Seeing as how Grandpa nearly absorbed the horns of one of his critters, Grandpa sensed he had an edge at the trial for Hezekiah had never spoke against Grandpa's wide load.

Next morning, he walked from his place to the road to head downhill to Hezekiah's courtroom. The morning sun was on time, but heavy cloud cover dragged thick blankets over every beam drilling into its denseness. It looked evening. Night lights were still on in the barn yards. Cars with blinding brights followed one another like ducklings over to Hezekiah's place. Judging by the parked cars, Deputy Duty worked a sleepless hundred and sixty-one hour week (one hour out a day to munch donuts over to the cafe). The question remained, should Grandpa drape his *bleep* with a red reflective triangle going down hill, or not? If not, he'd have to chance Duty sneaking up. Smarter than he looked, Grandpa cloaked his shoulders, back and front with a road construction vest that glowed like a lightning bug tail. He marched over to confront his accuser before the Union Township JP.

What was going on at Hezekiah's. An auction?

Everybody was heading into the barn, not the house. Hadn't Deputy Duty said the JP court convened today? No interest in an auction, Grandpa knocked on Hezekiah's kitchen door. The big man with ears corn cob long, a body rounder than a champion hog in bib overalls opened it, but seeing as how his mouth was stuffed with flapjacks, offered no greeting. The missus, her contorted face a rival to one who flew broomsticks, growled, "Scat! Courtroom's over to the barn." The door slammed shut.

Grandpa's feelings were hurt. He did right by Hezekiah forgetting his heifer was out to do the slicker a mischief, an now only to have the door slammed in his face. On the other hand, maybe Hezekiah would come to his senses when the flapjacks filled his innards. Perhaps then his judicial judgement would be sweeter when the wide load case was called for hearing?

Grandpa entered the barn. It dated back to homestead times. Where there had been a milking room, cheese-making room and a scullery, there were benches on which local folks silently sat holding Deputy Duty tickets. The tickets were held in hand like admission tickets for an usher to collect at the movie show. Grandpa reckoned he too was to sit on one of those benches and hold his ticket ready for the collection. With so many waiting to be called to the bench, he'd not get up there until the dawn of the twenty-second century, and the scenery the other side of the barn left a lot to be desired, looking all that time at the south side of dairy cows looking north. Where was the JP's bench? He looked around. Underneath the hay loft, the front seat of a Model A was perched on several hay bales. An antique creamer sat across from it, much like a desk.

The barking of a dog cut short curiosity when everybody else stood up, Grandpa a little later. Out of an old churning room came Hired Dog himself, and behind him, Hired Man. What was going on? It was Hired Man going on! Darned if he, like the ex-king of France, didn't get on the Model A seat. Climbing up and sitting at his right hand was Hired Dog acting the ex-king's ex-prime minister.

Hired Man, slamming a tin cream skinner on the desk, (it screamed), yelled as if deep in the lost forest, "Order in the court!" The robust call was uncalled for, silent as the folks were. Hired Man next grabbed the handle of an old back can. He lifted the lid and spat a huge gob therein, (as lawyer's say), clanging the lid shut just as if whatever went in had a mind to crawl back out. Luckily the can held about seven gallons. Grandpa wondered was Hired Man the bailiff? He couldn't be a JP dressed in Hezekiah's cast off coveralls unwashed from shoveling dung! "Bailiff," Hired Man snorted, "fetch the ticket of the first violator."

Danged if Hired Dog didn't leave and shuffle down to the flat stone floor, snickering like he did when Hezekiah told Grandpa the bull that attacked him was nothing but a heifer. Hired Dog stopped at Grandpa and his jaws snatched the ticket. (Hired dog's jaws, not Grandpa's). Hired Dog then ran the legal instrument back to the JP's bench.

Grandpa was ticked off and fit to suffer contempt of

court over the bailiff's snickering. Who would have figured Hired Dog was bailiff, Hired Man the JP!

"Approach the bench, Grandpa, Deputy Duty," Hired Man crowed. "What's this here wide load on about, Deputy?"

Duty said, honey on his words, "This old trout was swimming the fog of yesterday morning on the back road up to the old school house, like as not seen by any law abiding pickup, excepting there was a red reflective triangle on that there wide-e-e-e rump." Duty twisted his right arm way back so he could point out the focus of the law violation. "Didn't want to do no more than warn the old ham hock against getting a rusty radiator caught cheek tight, him not wearing a triangle. Changed my mind when the old coot lighted out like a buck on opening day."

"What you got to say on it, Grandpa?"

Grandpa was peeved it was told wrongly, but being uncertain which one, Hired Dog or Hired Man, had asked him to tell his side, Grandpa backed off throwing dirt on the Deputy. A defense came to mind. He'd face Hired Man, not snickering Hired Dog. If he were the JP, there would be grounds to take a guilty finding up to the next court level because Hired Dog was all animal, not rational. Then again, Hired Man rational? "First of all, your honor," he said, noting Hired Man swell up with pride, "any intelligent being," he was careful to talk broadly that Hired Dog assume he was included in 'intelligent', "knows I'm not a boxcar, a biplane, a tank or a sailing ship so I'm not excluded from the road. Right?" He got Hired Dog's nod of agreement. Hired Man's came after he'd thought on it. "That means if I'm not included in subsection (b) *a vehicle or other mode of transportation*, the definition of wide load doesn't apply to me. Right?" Hired Man hurried to nod agreement before Hired Dog did. "All intelligent people can see I'm not a vehicle. Right?" Agreeing nods were simultaneous. "That leaves other modes of transportation. If I'm not a mode of transportation, then wide load doesn't apply. Right?"

Hired Man said, "Got feet, don't you?"

"I do, your honor, as do the fine animals of Hezekiah the other side of the barn, their rump steaks lined up over there neat as ten pins in a bowling alley. Many a time I've seen that fine farmer and his skilled Hired Man herd them down the back road to school house hill's pasture."

"You're right there, Grandpa," Hired Man said. "I'm skilled, sure enough. Never lost me a critter the years I drove them up or brought them back."

"What you getting at, Geezer," Deputy Duty said, interrupting. He was upset Hired Man was going along with Grandpa.

"Demonstrable evidence!" Grandpa said, and ambled over to the display of backside beef on the hoof. One by one, he stood behind each critter wiggling his derriere. (Grandpa wiggled). "Close," he said, "but my hindquarters don't come up to the magnificence displacement of flesh of any of these fine cows. Right, Deputy?"

"How's that evidence?"

Grandpa was waiting on the question. "As his honor said, many times he drove these cows up and down the road to and from the old school house's pasture." Grandpa turned to face the man and dog on the Model A seat. "Your honor? Did you hang a red reflective triangle on any or all of those bottoms broader than the one I wiggled to the court?"

Eyes wider than Hired Dog's, Hired Man snorted, "Case dismissed. Bailiff, fetch the next ticket!"

HOLY SMOKE CHURCH SUPPER

The dust from the road flowed to the east after the half ton pickup pulled off and onto the cut grass where it grew thick from what feeding geese dropped from their other ends. Most times, way out in rural Union Township, a pickup's passing, dust and waiving hands or a finger to the left of the right index, was a day's event for Grandpa, a city slicker going to grass.

His callers were neighbors Hezekiah, dairy farmer, and his hired man, Homer. Hezekiah, at the wheel, took to hollering out the right side open window, no mind given to Hired Man's ear. "Hey Grandpa, it's tenderloin on the grill for supper tonight over to County Crossroads Church. Come along and join us!"

"Another Church supper?" Grandpa anticipated more needling. "Sure!" Before this neighborliness, he'd nearly become a fixture on his front porch reading clear through the Volumes until 29 of the 1911 Edition of Encyclopedia Britannica. He'd worried if his road walking exercise resumed, fleeing another horned critter might find diminishing returns. You see, out on the back road, it was Hezekiah's beef's jagged horns that were directed toward Grandpa's tender following. But for the woods' tree trunks, most as wide as Grandpa, nothing could have stayed the animal's injections. Telling Hezekiah his huge bull was up to mean mischief, Grandpa got not an ounce of sympathy. Rather, he was jollied not knowing it was a heifer. It made no difference there wasn't time to give a sex test to the assailing critter.

Grandpa had gone to a couple of church suppers on his own hoping to meet township folks not into funning him. Over to the basement of Pleasant Hills Church, where the ladies served chili and vegetable soup stirred by Quinta, her face as red as the soup's tomatoes, Hezekiah and Hired Man came on in. They chanted away to all folks far and near on Grandpa not knowing a heifer from a bull before sitting to pray with Pastor Round. Brightness of his new teeth a sun, he spread words of blessing over the food as if manuring crops. Then didn't he recall last week's sermon from1 Romans 26 associating it with the evils ongoing up in the north of Union township, she-ing and a'she-ing and he-ing and 'he-ing of unholy folks.

Grandpa muttered, "Pastor's so long winded chili's turned solid and soup's evaporated."

Hezekiah and Hired Man guffawed off their chairs to the dismay of proper folks.

At the all-you-can-eat ham and beans supper over to Pond Wood Church, Hezekiah and Hired Man showed up in clean bib overalls, and again chanted away to all folks far and near on Grandpa not knowing a heifer from a bull. They had to lull over a ham hock when Minister Mont took the podium and thanked the women cooking the food, gave his blessing, and like Pastor Round, took to preaching, mentioning 1 Corinthian 7: "Married folks from up north in Union Township ain't like us folks in Pond Wood. We marry rather than burn with lust."

When Grandpa asked Hezekiah and Hired Man just

where in the north of the township all this burning with lust was located, they giggled near to busting.

Come evening, Hezekiah pulled his pickup off the road on to grass and hollered. "My hired man and me be going now to County Crossroads Church, Grandpa. Follow on!"

He did, steering his pickup after Hezekiah's barreling half- ton that bounced off every rut. If they rolled over, no matter the flips, the remains of those big bodies in overalls, feet in manured boots, would never be beyond recognition.

Arriving safely, Hezekiah hurried on. A distance behind, Hired Man and Grandpa descended into Crossroads Church basement. A dozen hunters with orange caps were in line for tenderloin pot pie. The crew serving looked like parolees from a maximum security chow hall. Grandpa saw no women or kids. Where were they? Pot pie lumped high as a mole mound on plates, Grandpa and Hired Man sat down. Silence spread among the good old boys when one in a black robe draped from toe to neck, stood up. The Pastor? No blessing given, he went right to 25 Deuteronomy 11. "When two men get into a fight," he said, "and the wife of one comes to his aid and grabs the foe by his tender dangles, should she be punished?"

Hired Man hollered, "Yea! Cut off her hand without pity like the Good Book say."

The Preacher, Hezekiah it was, turned and pointed. "Is that why that there old slicker Grandpa never did say nothing about grabbing that there bull by its oysters."

Jocularity fell on Grandpa as thick as the pot pie crust he'd bent his fork on.

Next day an '83 pickup rattled Grandpa's driveway stone. Out its door emerged a primal creature looking a stuffed green pepper in combat boots, a woman a couple of decades short of a hundred, eye glasses pinching her nostrils.

Grandpa met her at the side door. "Ma'am," he said, "are you lost?"

"No siree," she said. "I be calling with this here sweet potato pie. Covered it against bugs come in from the beans." She pointed with milking fingers long as asparagus stalks. "My boy Homer be Hezekiah's hired man. I be upset when he tell me Hezekiah near split his sides from the funning on you over to Crossroads Church, you being a slicker and all."

"Nice of you, Ma'am," he said. "Please come in. I'll put on coffee and cut the pie."

"I be called Delicta,' she said, coming in. "Can't stay but a flip of a fly's wings. About putting an end to the funning, here's how to tie Hezekiah to his own manure spreader." She stepped two rungs up on the kitchen stool and leaned on Grandpa's left ear. He tried not to flinch, though he was onto the fact his good looks were the long side of a volcano's blown slope, his body run down as a roofless barn. Even so, a kiss? It wasn't. It was whispering, her breath moist and warm as coffee vapor. "That'll churn Hezekiah's fireplace for sure," she said climbing down, then winking her droopy left eye lid. She left Grandpa with pie and an alliance.

The line for tickets up in north Union Township's Holy Smoke church's annual fish fry was longer than one at the dollar double feature Saturday matinee. Hezekiah, shined boots, scrubbed bib overalls on and his best cap adorning his balding head, was of a mind to depart, excepting he was Grandpa's invite. Taking note a pretty woman was selling tickets and others waiting tables, not to pay mind to sissy looking fellows at the serving table, Hezekiah wondered if they were the she-ing and a'she-ing and the he-ing and 'a'he-ing folks Pastor Round spoke on, or Pastor Mont's folks who didn't marry to hamper lust. Never mind, Hezekiah reflected. He was a righteous man fearless in any den of iniquity.

"Welcome," said ticket seller Lotta to Grandpa and his guest. "Two?" Her smile was dazzling, white blouse as crisp as a Thanksgiving's table clothe. She sat at a card table, took cash and doled out passes.

Grandpa and Hezekiah moved along the line for a paper plate, napkin and plastic dinnerware before reaching cafeteria style tables. Those young fellows who served food wore jeans near to squeeze their grapes to wine, cheery smiles and rubber gloves to dish out potato chips and massive pieces of hot fried fish. Next was Hired Man's mama, Delicta, who asked folks to choose from an assortment of pie slices and drinks, hot coffee, milk or kool-aid. Judging from kids' mustaches, kool-aid was orange flavored.

Tables were loaded with loaves of brown and white

bread, butter dishes, plates of sliced tomatoes and green peppers, bowls of tartar sauce. People filled the seven rows of end to end dining tables that ran from the serving tables to the back of the basement. The bathrooms were there. Late comers sat at row ends! Chow-hounds, family and friends, hunkered down at tables closest to the serving line to devour all the fried fish they could before those waiting in line cleaned out the balance. Those in line hollered for them to leave some. It was an annual fear.

Grandpa found middle seats. Appealing young waitresses carrying hot and cold liquids or heaping plates of hot fried fish came on with refills. Some fish swallowers talked, others chewed, chewers leading talkers. Hezekiah wasn't a talker, chewing, like to stave off famine, on fried fish slopped with tartar sauce.

Delicta ambled over. "Nice of you boys to come all the way from south township. Holy Smoke be my church."

"Sure's good fish," Hezekiah said between bites.

"Have more," she said, calling to a fellow from the serving line.

Now to say that fellow walked dainty wasn't a mockery, seeing as he skipped like a ten year old girl over to Hezekiah to dish up a big hunk of fish. Then didn't the sissy boy lift off Hezekiah's cap to kiss the farmer's rumpled scalp.

"You're so sweet," Dainty said, skipping off.

Hezekiah took on the shade of a boiled lobster

"Pay him no mind, he be just too nice," Delicta said.

The south township man was of a mind he was, for sure, in a den of iniquity. What a story he had to tell Pastors Pound and Mont. If only he'd Grandpa's keys to his pickup, he'd be a skedaddling there right now. Hot wiring crossed his mind, but he'd not fall to wrong.

"Sure gave you a right good looking hunk of fish, Hezekiah," Delicta said, "eat up."

"Dang thing won't cut," he said, jabbing it with a fork. It bounced off the plate like a ball. He watched it jump. "Be it carp?"

Then Lotta, the ticket taker, appeared beside him. She looked a run-way model in a tuck-stitch cardigan, white blouse and black classic trousers. His mouth flew open, eyes puckered. The white edge of her shirt outlined a tanned neck and face, eyes blue and bright. He looked into those eyes, fantasizing. She leaned on him, left arm around his neck, her breath flower sweet.

"I'm like the wife in 25 Deuteronomy 11," she said as her right hand edged down Hezekiah's overalls.

"Holy smoke," he hollered, no action taken to divert the roving hand.

Delicta hooted, letting out a bellow that turned heads.

Folks around the tables joined the hilarity, reckoning south township's Hezekiah was this year's dupe, hoaxed by Lotta, the rubber buffalo fish, and the football team's star quarterback.

"Got me," Hezekiah said, grimacing the smile of the duped.

FRISKY CARP

Homer, the hired man, stopped Grandpa walking down hill near the entry to Hezikiah's dairy farm to brag on the big carp he caught the other day and took over to Mama Delicta's.

He said, "Besides that there jumbo I hauled in, there's nigh on more as big down by the base of the stream in the wetlands. Matter of fact, there be over a thousand different kinds of carp I be knowing of, and maybe a half a hundred more if I don't lose my count of the carps swimming over to the pond at the Chinese 'All You Can Eat'."

Who, other than Homer, was going to count assorted carp when there was beef, chicken, stuffed mushrooms, egg rolls and baked salmon fresh cooked and hot when carried out of Wong's kitchen?

"There ain't a taste in the whole of the wide world can compete with fried carp after Mama puts a hot skillet under it." Homer said, continuing his updating. "Carps have a air bladder connected to the ear by a chain of small bones. They chew in the gullet where cavity bones have teeth that work food against a hard plate."

Knowing nothing about carp before Homer's chattering never bothered Grandpa, nor did getting to know about them rank right up there with the out come of the County Jail guards baseball game against Union Township's asphalt crew.

None the less, Grandpa remained a polite listener.

"There be four sub-families of carp in North America," Homer said. "They live in lakes, ponds, canals, slow-running streams where there's plenty of greenery. They eat greenery, worms, small animals that fall in. The book says, carps came from Asia and got to England in 1496. I got it written right here on my thumb." He looked at the left thumb. "Christopher Columbus was over in 1492, so it must have been them Quakers brought carps to America in the Mayflower."

"You think so?" Grandpa said to pretend interest.

"Seeing as you can keep a secret," Homer said, then leaned on Grandpa's good left ear to whisper, "I'm a going to show you where them carps grow big as hogs down in the wetland. "Come on."

Now Homer had Grandpa's curiosity as high as his blood pressure.

They walked from Hezikiah's graveled road entry and crossed the township road Grandpa traversed most every day west and east, then east and west to get fit, though fitness was a long way off. Homer led into the wetlands over to the stream where water flowed after leaving the ditch through Hezikiah's cow pasture. They followed the stream toward Lake Maxinkuckee, walking through dense vegetation, residences for noisy creatures of air, land, and stream.

Coming to a pool, Homer held back his follower. "Look," He said pointing to where water was flying, reeds were waving.

There wasn't much of a breeze, yet the water was percolating like a coffee pot on a fire.

"What's going on down there?" Grandpa said, eyes back in their sockets.

"Carps be mating," he said.

"Mating?" Grandpa was flabbergasted. One never knew all about one's neighbors. He hadn't an idea Homer took to fish pornography. Yet Grandpa hesitated to convict the hired man before all the evidence was in. He'd cross examine. "How do you know they're mating? To me, they're fighting, acting crazy."

"Them male carps ain't crazy!" Homer said. "Water's fresh, air's hot, plants be growing, so the female carps gets all worked up. Male carps smell worked up girl carps and get after them. That's when fighting comes on. Carp males be fighting for carp females. That be why the water's flying. Look at them big old carp males messing up each other, then the winners rubs up carp females, body to body. Them carp girls take the hint. They lay eggs in the water, then thrash around in circles in the floating reeds to move their eggs. Them carp males ooze out milt with sperm and fertilize thousands of them eggs."

"Carp copulation," Grandpa said, rejecting the thought Homer had a bent to fish porno.

"Don't rightly know about 'carp cops'," Homer said, "but them eggs hang onto grasses. That's where they grow up."

"How big?"

"Maybe four to five feet, fifty to sixty pounds. Look

39

at that big carp over there."

Grandpa followed the point and saw what looked to be a dolphin. The carp had a large dorsal fin, lines of large scales side by side and what looked like barbels each side of the mouth. "It would take a derrick to haul that one to shore."

"Foul them with sharp hooks," Homer said. "Going back to get it. There ain't a taste in the whole of the wide world can compete with fried carp after Mama puts a hot skillet under it."

Grandpa kept it to himself wetland's carp fed by greenery that flourished in waters that passed through Hezikiah's pasture manured by tons of dairy cow droppings, no mattered it went into Mama Delicta's skillet, most certainly tasted unlike any fried fish served up at St. Mary's church suppers.

He said nothing about it, staying nice.

RETIRING OUT TO UNION TOWNSHIP

Here's how Grandpa came out to Union Township. When he was on to retiring, Grandma was on to thinking about moving from the big city out to the country. Grandpa wasn't on to it much. He told her this well known fact of country aging: 'if you don't die, you're going to get older.' Getting older for folks out in the country locked into Medicare meant a need to find a medical type on that payment scale who would squeeze an arm, poke a vein and write in Egyptian what would cure an ailment.

Not to mention emergency medical services!

When Grandma set her mind, it was in concrete. So they went about looking. Where to hang out the years until the last sunrise? There were small towns in Union Township and others south of the county line. So Grandpa took it on himself first to check out the towns over the other side of the toxic waste dump, closed for not doing the right thing with dumped poisons. Driving along side an abandoned railway, he dodged pickups leaping out of dirt runways surrounded by rusting hulks of pickup parts growing tall weeds. He hadn't an idea rusting pickup parts were good fertilizer, or was it dog droppings underneath? Other pickups gunned past the only stop sign in town. Houses were worn out, trailers feeble. Zoning wasn't a local word. A revved pickup spun gravel where a lone tavern was open. If there were medical talent inside, which side of the bar? Grandpa moved on.

Next town still had residential neighborhoods, a Carnegie library, churches, a long closed railroad hotel, a police station, post office, a spirited café and a lit up tavern down the road from a closed medical clinic, except from two to four on Mondays and Thursdays if birthing mothers called in advance. Grandpa marveled over how those mothers could time that. A long abandoned and decaying two story red brick building embodied the decomposing zest of the town's main street.

Grandpa found no joy in the demise of small rural towns, but he understood why folks held out in the back acres. They, and he, enjoyed the beauty of landscapes across rural fields, farms and woods. Brown reeds tall as palisades of Indian forts guarded wetlands. A gaggle of geese flying a 'V' called in an untranslatable language. An abandoned, weathered corral chute peeked from bushy captors. Birds in a flight group, some wearing raspberry bibs, caught the eye. Big pure bred Holsteins fed on bigger bales of hay. Did a thousand pound animal void twelve tons of manure annually? That was big time voiding!

Over to Culver in Union Township, Grandpa informed Grandma, there was a Doctor whose name was Irish and the Doc's family name was included in the ancient Irish Annals of the Kingdom of Ireland, written by the Four Masters. What better medical credential was needed? As glad as he was that there was a Doc, what if he or Grandma were to have clouded eyes, dizziness, headaches, retching, passing out? Could Union Township's

Emergency Medical Service fetch the ill one from deep in the township to a hospital within a few hours, the window needed to get stroke-busting drugs, if that was what ir was, to have the best chance of avoiding disability?

If Grandpa or Grandma needed an ambulance run out to the country, how long the run? If he needed a run to a hospital, how long? While his aging body was still numbered among the surviving elderly, before Grandma made an offer on a farm house with three acres, there was time to look up the township's ambulance outfit. It was top rate, but those EMS boys wouldn't be driving their pickups. The ambulance was a hulk of a truck that called for tender loving locomotion all the while the alarm shrieked. Good as those boys might be moving the hulk south on roads snaking around the lake's cottages, the minutes Grandpa's 1986 sedan used doing the same was past eighteen. If he'd slowed on curves, it would have been past twenty-one.

What about a hospital run? Way up north and east in the county's big town, there was one. Pushing his sedan to its limit north, he ran the roads snaking the lake, then up the winding highway to the big town. Thirty-seven minutes, not counting the minutes the ambulance ran out to his place. With cars speeding all the way, Grandpa came right on down to this conclusion: Grandma's wish for a place out in the country met the time frame for possible survival.

So Grandma's wanting a place way out in Union Township went down easily. And what a place! The farm house's field stone foundation held up clapboard siding like that of the nineteenth century. Out front was a long and deep screened porch painted as white as the house. On the west side, a three sided turret rose from field stone. On the first floor front was a double light Gothic window with tall but narrow single light windows on either side. A double window to the rear opened the kitchen. On the second floor was a double window similar to the kitchen's. A large living room on the east side ran from the front to the back of the house with a west dining room and kitchen down. Upstairs, there were three bedrooms and a bathroom. Old farmers built outhouses fifty feet out on a back quarter acre. Later generations built with that luxury on the second floor for drainage and extra airing a wind might allow.

A flower and vegetable garden bore scent and food. Four thick vines, each one crawling like a python up a leg of a steel tower branched in all directions on a windmill. The pythons met at the top and choked thin steel slats to stillness. June through August the vines' dark green leaves brought forth hundreds of clusters of long showy orange-red trumpets, as if serenading the sun. If Grandpa listened closely he'd see hummingbirds, as if on restless wheels, whirl. Birds of all feathers hid beneath the leaves, warbling, shrilling, jibing, mourning. Their melodies lingered. In October, long brown seed pods, as if pre-Christmas decorations, dangled from stringy branches.

Sitting on his redwood chair on the front porch, Grandpa recollected, back in the city, ambulances were slowed by heavy traffic. Emergency rooms were so crowded quick attention was a low number, just as if at a meat market. Though the ambulance out to his place in

Union Township took time, he figured viewing the wetlands and swallowing an aspirin or two might tide him over until EMS did what they could.

If it didn't work, cows and critters would moan for him.

DOINGS OF NATURE AND MAN

Grandpa used to walk tiny strips of concrete called sidewalks back in the city. They was wide as a cat's left whisker. Often, desperadoes no bigger than dandelions with hair as fuzzy would come out from behind tree trunks to throw up road blocks. Tough little tykes made their play backed by water guns. Buy a nickel glass of lemonade, nasty tasting stuff, or get a face full. Them little people were in training for big time sales careers, being as their expenses were met by the neighbor's outdoor faucet water and penny packets of yellow stuff, Mom floating a loan at interest. (Hers, as long as them tykes stayed out the house and played!)

Grandpa, favoring a pay off rather than sticky stuff in his hair, what little clung to the pavement called scalp, would pop the nickel (it was long ago when a nickel was something) and take one of them paper cups full. Out of sight, he'd sterilize the city's fire hydrants. Tiny mites wasn't the worst hazard of Grandpa's city walking. Drivers, State licensed looneys with cell phone in hand behind wheels with frosted windows of motorized elephants blowing steel splitting trumpets, and worse, voiding thick smog that turned nature's flowers to plastic, (now you know where all them plastic flowers in grave yards come from) took no notice of nothing. Sometimes city Cops gave tickets to the tailing car in the jet stream of rampaging smog, but mostly to Grandpa for jay walking. Wouldn't say he took them kindly, accused as he was of (1) messing with the flow of speeding cars, (2) causing the smog to linger over the street where policemen flashed radar guns (it was really long ago), and (3) provoking drivers into blasting horns and interrupting cell phone's sweet talk. (Why else had them elephant mouths a need to talk at forty-five in a twenty mile an hour traffic zone?)

Moving from the city to back acres where sidewalk ain't a word in the Union Township annual budget and the voiding of motorized elephants near extinct, (pickups are more like groundhogs), Grandpa found time to gaze and observe the doings of the wide country-side, movable and fixed. He felt safe afoot on roads long forgotten by the County's road crews. (Why, one of them County tractors cutting road side jungle weeds got lost under the falling foliage! Grandpa, going about an act of mercy as he was, stifled his temper at the hired dog's everlasting snickering over the bull turned heifer incident, just to rent him to sniff out the tractor driver.)

The slow slope from Grandpa's place down to the swamp turned a stairway to the sky on the way back up. He mourned like a dove going up hill, but the looking was good. The road was lined with tall pines, growing corn, reeds that lined either side of the swamp's creek like palisades an Indian fort, and on the opposite side of the culvert, bred Holsteins. They were big as hay bales stacked out of reach over by the line fence. Contented, they paid no mind to the wanderer. Calves did. They frolicked like butterflies. Next fenced field over, yearlings in a line turned heads together as if hinged to study the two legged critter walking where grass didn't grow. There was close on to a hundred of them black and white critters in the dairy herd. Not a one of them was on a cell phone, or racing to beat the next red light, or spewing a trail of discolored chemicals.

Grandpa turned his attention to the swamp. (Town folks called it a wetland). That there swamp was actually a church for the survivors of man's never ending development of the land where there was water deeper than city basements' quarter inch. There was green on the swamp water, mallard ducks and ducklings cutting trails. Canadian geese winged in. Hundreds bobbed on the liming lake. Swamp birds sung prettily like the Silvertones barber-shoppers over to the Indiana State fair. City birds weren't so musical, but that was when city nature wasn't nothing but sewer rats. A squirrel on a limb was ticked. A relative lost a race. If death was at night, them little litter bearers of the dark would have remove the remains. Sanitation was big in the woods. Critters can't win no twenty foot dash on a State road where pickups speed to outrun the Township Tax Assessor! Wild apple and pear trees lined the road, running south like Midwest manufacturing. A deer stood silently in alfalfa, snorted and waved a white tail 'so long' while crossing the road. It was a beautiful creature but with the brains of a bird's nest. If a pickup happened by, she'd hit it fender high; usually a night game.

Maple leaves, green on the north, were rust colored south. Grandpa remembered the herbicide truck working the fields in May. Its stuff laid dormant the weeks of no rain, but come the howling south winds kicking up earth like dust bowl times and then the cloudburst, it freed the power of them chemicals to devour leaves.

It was more an act of man than nature. That thought hit Grandpa higher on his head than his crossed-eyes! Nature's deposits versus Man-made! Grandpa got on to thinking on it.

Dairy farmer Hezikiah told him a thousand pound cow voided twelve tons a year! (Grandma used more than that on her tomatoes.) At that, voiding was in direct balance to the amount of milk a cow produced. Milk out-put was tied to the animal's food eating. As often as Hezekiah drove the back roads to the barn with newly cut hay, his cows were fat and well-spent all over the pasture. Limited to ten fingers and nine toes, Grandma's more or less, Grandpa went over to the school house. Teacher Oscar let it be known one hundred cows times twelve tons of voidance were two million four hundred thousand pounds. Even Grandma admitted that was a lot of fertilizer! Why, she could cover every city garden in the old neighborhood with enough left to fill both the City and County Council chambers back there, and Culver's too, except Culver's councilpersons already accomplished it.

Sure enough, conservationists took unkindly to Hezikiah's cows dropping so much reflexive pollination on just a hundred acres the other side of the culvert! They said it fouled the swamp which drained into the lake. Grandpa never got an answer to the question why faraway runoff of a hundred cows was considered pollution but the direct deposits of five times as many ducks and geese, nature! And where was them conservationists when, south of the county line, big city corporations handling out-of-state toxic waste for big dollars entered contracts underwriting the operator's cash flow, funding the digging and operation of a toxic waste dump. The dump got out of hand, sure enough. Its operator bailed out of responsibility for clean up through bankruptcy. The big city corporations hid behind mamas' corporate veils saying clean up wasn't their responsibility.

Grandpa wished corporations were up to the straight on doings of a striped skunk he ambled onto. She came out of tall grass followed by five dinky dittos, took a look at the worried face, arched her back, raised her tail and shuffled backwards. Expecting no kick in the shins, Grandpa evacuated just in time to get out of the line of fire of her acrid, blinding spray.

Not so lucky are folks who draw water from county line wells. They can't see the skunks and don't know where the line of flow of their acrid, toxic waste soup is heading.

The doings of nature ain't up to poisons of man!

LOST HIS WHISTLE

Grandpa, sitting in a lounge chair on his screened in front porch, often took to whistling a lip symphony to the critters of the back acres. Among them in Union Township were farmers Noah, Hezikiah, Homer the Hired Man and his best pal, Hired Dog. When bailing alfalfa across the road, they dallied to hear the melodious warbles radiating from Grandpa's lips, not counting the times he snorted his jug of Yukon Jack. Had to wet his whistle, hadn't he!

Grandpa marveled he could stir a Cardinal up in a maple tree. The male would hop from his mate's nest down limbs to find the intruder. Needed to size him up, never the wiser Grandpa wasn't a bird, though some said his brain was. Each attack flight to pluck the tuft off the scarlet pate was deflected by a trampoline screen, the bird bouncing like a gymnast.

But all great musical instruments need repair, so too Grandpa's after seven decades. On the lower lip's left side bulged a knoll a pathologist confirmed was carcinoma. A partial excision did the deed, the surgeon stitching the 'V' cleft to close the lip cut. Another scar? So what! It wasn't any more noticeable than the others of Grandpa's facial foot tracks.

Recuperation ongoing, he welcomed callers Noah, Hezikiah, and Hired Man to the front porch, seats on stuffed chairs and long drags on the jug of Yukon Jack. Hired Dog, a bit miffed at exclusion from porch and Yukon

Jack, barked, which reminded Homer of Grandpa's whistling. Then didn't he ask the old coot to whistle up a Cardinal?

Grandpa inhaled and blew. He hissed like an vexed snake. What? Another breathe taken, he blew from puckered lips. A hiss! Again and again, puckers and panting breaths but no whistle, only hisses calibrated for stump political speeches! Where was his whistle?

In a voice lower than a frog's belly, Grandpa said, "I've lost my whistle!"

"You sure ain't lost your bad breath," said Noah.

Ignoring the dig, Grandpa said, "must be that cutting on my lip."

"You going to apply for disability, Grandpa?" Hezikiah said.

"You're handicapped, sure enough!" Homer the Hired Man said.

"Handicapped?" answered Grandpa, "you listen." Eyebrows rising, mouth inhaling, air departing, nought but hisses vented.

"Handicapped for sure," said Hezikiah, snorting.

Grandpa had a flash of inspiration. "I wonder if Doc's malpractice insurance covers lost whistles?"

"Knowing you, Grandpa," Noah said, "from now on when you go to the big town's super store, you'll look for parking spots the other side of handicaps and pregnant mothers, the ones for 'Lost Whistlers.'"

"Trouble with that is," Hezikiah said, "when Grandpa goes to park in a lost whistler spot, along will come a pregnant lady who lost her whistle."

"Maybe there's a medicine to cure a lost whistle," said Noah, "like viagra."

"Viagra never did me no good," Homer the Hired Man said. "I can't whistle nothing!"

"Time to get back to the fields," Noah said.

Leaving, the farmers took to whistling the theme from 'Bridge Over the River Kwai'!

STUFFED OLIVE

Grandpa looked forward to help out the overburdened ombudsman by visiting the old folks over to Union Township nursing home. It would be like visiting the township library, except not checking out bound books, but meeting with skin-covered codgers eager to make impressions through the telling of tall tales.

He kicked over the moody motor of his pickup, its radio busted and motor moaning the short drive. He concentrated on dodging pickups leaping out from cow paths; pickups gunning through the town's four-way stop signs; pickups moving out of the lot of Seldom Closed Tavern.

He parked across the street from the nursing home. He'd driven by before, but was this building the same one he'd seen? Three circular wings and an extruding stem? It looked like a pawn shop symbol. He questioned the manhood of the architect.

Entry was barred at the gate of Union Township nursing home. Standing the other side of the glass door was a short great-grandma, face sea wave wrinkled, round body captured in a tight green dress. She tugged the door's handle inwardly holding on as if it were the last lifeboat in the Atlantic. She shook a thin mop of a reddish wig negatively to chase off the huge barbarian at the gate.

Grandpa saw a stuffed green olive.

He thought a smile could turn the crocodile from its

meal. It worked. Stuffed Olive let loose of the door handle. Carefully Grandpa opened it to face a pike waiting to attack prey.

She screeched, "I told my daughter not to see you anymore." The words echoed the narrow hall. Her index finger turned a dagger at his throat.

Grandpa blinked, but figured on it. Who ever was the beau Stuffed Olive was condemning wasn't him, and who on earth her daughter had been, he hadn't an awareness. He rolled with the jabs and verbal right crosses. Physical mildness belied his mental irritation at this dose of old timer anger.

"Your daughter dumped me," he said, imagination percolating, face mournful as a funeral director's, "like you wanted her to do. She's just too good for me." A weary expression confirmed it.

"She's a good girl, she is!" Stuffed Olive said. "She's too good for the likes of a scoundrel like you, leaving her that way." Nods of the red wig confirmed it. She retracted her dagger. Her wig settling like a blanket on a sleeping baby.

"Indeed she is a good girl," he said, sighing. Scoundrel? Left the family way?

"Ugliest baby ever I saw, shithead!" Stuffed Olive overly exaggerated her emphasis on 'shithead.' She clasped her tired thin hands as if to pray away illegitimacy.

Grandpa moved on into the nursing home wings. He figured old Stuffed Olive had quite a tale to tell, but danged if he'd stay to hear it!

UPGRADING THE COMMODE'S DRAIN FIELD

Old city slicker Grandpa took good to country living out to Union Township. Not so to his septic system. Its gurgling got him off his, aw, on to his feet to call in Septic Slurp.

Nearest waste water treatment plant was over to town and did only unto town people. Folks out in the Township voted against taxes for the running of pipes to the back acres, being as they were into free outhouses. Seeing as Township Trustee Green then took it on himself to oppose dropped loads spread over plowed fields, folks upgraded to flushing into septic systems.

Dairy farmer Hezikiah, though he came upon his farmstead from Great Granddad, (the inheritance weren't of value like them oil folks' kin), done set up Septic Slurp to get into the care and handling of neighbors' droppings. He'd refitted a truck with a ten thousand gallon tank, vacuum pump and hoses to tickle tank bottom sludge. Having no blossomed seed to call his own, he trained Homer, his Hired Man to do the slurping.

When not otherwise handling Grandpa's gurgles, come each April and October, Hired Man and his best pal, Hired Dog, came on to Grandpa's three acres. For a fee, of course, Homer would back the rig to position, run out the hose, put it in the tank and kick the pump to life. Like a straw in a chocolate soda, it slurped the collected cache.

Grandpa was always of a mind to abet. However, the time he brought the garden hose over for Homer's cleaning up only to see the hose disappear into the tank to spray around, then pulled out, tilted up, and a drink taken, abetting was over.

Not many months later, sitting on the porch looking north, a reek from the south molested Grandpa's nostrils. Following the foulness to the septic drain field he saw a bubbling. Crude? Crude alright, but not the kind oiling pickup motors. He called Septic Slurp

Hezikiah, Hired Man and Hired Dog were out quicker than the chipmunk out of his tunnel draining the bubbling. Over at the stink, Hezikiah got to pondering a while, then said, "this here bubbling's a bit removed from the house, Grandpa. Ain't no one gonna know". He looked down slope. "Seeing as there be a quarter mile betwixt your place and mine, and what with my herd voiding whenever they want all over the pasture, I ain't on to being bothered."

"That's big of you," Grandpa said, "but my bubbling is overriding your herd's smell."

"I suppose something clogged this old worn out system," Hezikiah said. "You see Grandpa, water from the house, be it from the toilet, sink and washing machine, flow out to the chambers with the yellow and brown mixing with the other waters. Most of the brown settles to the bottom where them bacteria eat on it. What sludge's left is pumped out by the slurping, so the yellow can go on. Not when the pipes be clogged. Them bacteria can chomp only so much. If'en the yellow flowed in the pipes and out to the drain field, it'd trickle through them drain pipes into the ground. Roots of plants eat up them nutrients left, clean it right good. Waters from the drain field, filtered by the dirt below, flow as clean to the water table as it did out of your well to the kitchen faucet."

Hezikiah's face turned pitiful. "Now off to town where they got one of them fancy treatment plants with all them trickling ponds and whatever, they do separate the brown from the yellow and most of the run off from the roads, houses, factories and stores. The solid stuff them bacteria leave behind be called 'residuals'. Don't know why. And it's a pity the town don't pump the treated water to a drain field to trickle into dirt for a final cleaning. They don't let the dirt eat up what ain't been fully cleaned. 'Stead, they pump it into the river to dilute where the town water works draws drinking water. Sad!"

Face turned sunny again, Hezikiah said, "Need a new septic system, Grandpa. A thousand gallon tank, drain field and all, cost you about two thousand."

"Go ahead," said Grandpa, impressed with Hezikiah's talk on clean water.

Within the week, Township Trustee Green was there for government supervising, Hezikiah and Homer moved equipment in and got right to the digging of a deep hole. No mind was paid to Hired Dog's gnawing on a mastodon bone. The Trustee weren't of no help, neither, seeing as he was chawing about the town sewage treatment team challenging others at the Waste Water Bowl.

Waste Water Bowl? Grandpa wondered on it. He'd

heard of the Super Bowl, the Rose Bowl, even the Sugar Bowl, but a Waste Water Bowl? Town Team? What trophy? A toilet bowl?

Trustee Green got to hollering 'watch out' all around when the concrete septic tank big as a mausoleum was lowered into the deep hole. Hezikiah, up out of the hole, got into a parley with Trustee Green about that there waste water bowl, the Trustee dropping sayings like 'headworks', 'filters', 'dewatering', 'digesters', 'clarifiers', 'rotating contractors'.

Homer weren't of a mind to speak digging a trench to the house from the west side.

Grandpa went to quiet thinking on the athletic events at the waste water bowl. A hundred meter relay swim in the collection pool? High jumping the bio-reactors? Broad jumping the sludge drying bed? A hundred meter dash along side the oxidation ditch? Pole vaulting the pump station? Butterfly relays? Shot putting? A mile relay? What was the baton? The shot?

Hezikiah revved up his backhoe and got to digging a trench from the east side to where Homer was on to digging a series of parallel trenches, placing in each a long drain pipe. He connected the pipe from the house's plumbing to the tank and from the tank to the drain field's pipes. Wounds in the ground were filled in and smoothed out.

"Good work," said Trustee Green. "Everything meets standards, Hezikiah. You and Homer done a right good job. I'll send my report on to the county. Hey,

Grandpa," he said. "About that there waste water bowl over to town. Be tomorrow morning about eight. The boys are going to cheer our team."

"We'll fetch you," Hezikiah said.

Nex morning, Grandpa felt out of place in Hezikiah's pickup not wearing bib overalls and Hired Dog preferring his lap to Homer's. Over to the treatment plant, a passel of men, dressed like going to work in a mill, ambulated into an office building, athletes no doubt, going to register for the events. Were the older men coaches or athletes? So many were up the decade scale, Grandpa came to think youngsters took unkindly to butterflying in a wastewater lagoon. Admiration soared for the teams of old goats challenging each other in field events.

Danged if challenges had a thing to do with slushing around in sewage on the fields of play. Sewage treatment teams tested knowhow, not biceps, during five events, like planing a field for applying bio-solids; repairing a pump to slush sewage through the treatment workings.

Grandpa was impressed with their learned minds, Hezikiah and Homer dismayed over the lack of sludge slinging.

UNION TOWNSHIP WEEKLY
LOCALS LOSE WASTE WATER BOWL

Yesterday, deep in the bowels of the sewage plant, several teams loosened up for the challenge ahead in the Waste Water Bowl. The town's well-oiled team was there in competition with area teams to test the skills needed to operate treatment of raw sewage.

Most of us take for granted liquids flow from draining bathtubs, sinks, washing machines, toilets, rain runoff, snow melt, factory and stores through pipes beneath town to its treatment plant. Most times it does, so what happens once the water gets there?

A waste water plant is an engineered design that handles the daily influx of waste water from initial inflow to discharge. A walk through finds a bar screen keeps out sticks and large objects, a chamber collects grit and sand, a primary clarifier separates water and sludge, water moving on, sludge down. Bacteria in aeration basins trickling filters remove dissolved components in the water. Secondary clarifiers take up where the primary clarifier left off. The waste is removed from the initial inflow waters. As for sludge, it goes through an anaerobic (no oxygen) enclosed digester and a vacuum filter to remove all water. The de-watered residue becomes fertilizer.

What about our team? They told all of us, this Weekly reporter, Union Township dairy farmer Hezikiah and Homer, his Hired Man, that they numbered among the highly qualified staff that know the operational details behind bar screens (devices to lacerate sticks, paper), oxidation ditches (oval channels with aeration, air, devices), air flotation (separating suspended matter from wastewater), sedimentation (removal of solids that settled during primary clarification and biomass during secondary clarification), sludge digestion (sludge removed during primary clarification in aerobic treatment and later during anaerobic, no air, sludge digesters), trickling filters (the dosing of wastewater over rock or plastic pieces), and lastly, but not including every procedure, activated carbon treatment (absorbing toxic substances like metals and pesticides).

Our teams' knowledge wasn't as expansive as their mouths. They knew an updated average and peak hours flow rate was necessary to compute to be ready for heavy rains and snow melts. They added wrongly. They knew organic matter in water will naturally decay as a result of the presence of microorganisms in the receiving body of water before some team member's bottle of whiskey slipped out of pocket into the soup, so trickling filters that encouraged bacteria to grow rapidly in a waste water environment and act as the primary agents of treatment slowed way down. Our men knew the mixing of microorganisms with sewage and oxygen supplied by aeration in the first clarifier digests organics, and by moving it to the next clarifer, separates water from sludge, but our team cut off the air. They knew how to best utilize this residue to safely fertilize farm fields, but only Union Township crop farmer Noah said he'd take it.

Next year, hopefully, our dead last boys will upgrade their knowledge and procedural abilities, and live up to the backing of loyal fans like Hezikiah, proprietor of Septic Slurp, and his Hired Man, Homer. Neither of them good ole boys were any too happy paying off bets.

UNION TOWNSHIP POLITICS

The Executive Committee of the Union Township nursing home's Resident Council took Grandpa's advice, (he was a volunteer helper to the ombudsman), to invite the candidates for the Township Trustee's job. Though Grandpa had pulled seventy-five years and was nearly on a par with pickup hulks out to the salvage yard, all that walking he'd done over the last ten years had kept him the out side of twenty-four hour inside care. The invites accepted, the walls of the dining room were littered with political posters and enlarged photos of candidates for Township Trustee. Ollie Oddle was the candidate with canoes for lips. Jake Berry looked a prize-size gourd.

The debate turned off even alert folks, particularly when angry Ollie said, 'I'm a candidate for Trustee, Oscar, and I don't take kindly to you repeating them vulgar noises.'

Old Oscar, one of the residents, twitched a lot in his wheel chair, but he didn't mean to trumpet gas, at least the first two times. More than one other resident tooted in sympathy.

Afterwards, Grandpa suggested the Executive Committee call a meeting to discuss the candidates' merits, if any.

Gladys did so, and as council president, held the right to have Grandpa push her wheelchair head of the line into the activities room. A convoy of wheelchairs holding

Mabel, Narcissa and Floyd followed. All rolled to places around the short end of the long bingo table.

Grandpa pulled over a chair to chime in, if invited. He took notice the women were dressed like Old Amish sheep, that all remembered the end of World War I. Floyd wore bib-overalls, a farmer most of last century except for World War II's battlefields where he fired a 1917 A1 Browning Machine Gun. He hadn't forgotten the hard life of farming; the women, the harder life of marriages to farmers.

Fingers fish hooks from arthritis, Gladys avoided a gavel. "I call the committee to order. What about the Trustee race? Is Ollie or Jake leading?"

"Ollie isn't leading here at our place," Narcissa said, veins on her neck fluttering, "seeing how he embarrassed Oscar."

"My son tells me to vote for the best man," Floyd said. His crystal ball of a head glowed.

Mabel, the long ago one room school teacher with fingers long as rulers, corrected him. "There's just two candidates, Floyd. "It's, 'my son tells me to vote for the BETTER man.'"

"Batter?" The ringing in Floyd's ears still reproduced the sounds of incoming German 88 rounds. "Your son or mine couldn't hit a lick on the Union Township baseball team."

Gladys cut off Mabel's reply. "Who won the Ollie versus Jake debate?"

Mabel said, "If Ollie and Jake, instead of debating,

65

got into a pitchfork fight, from what I hear from folks who know the two, no one would intervene."

"Be that as it may," Gladys said, "who won the debate?"

Narcissa said, "Why was there a debate in the first place? Who listens to Ollie trying to out talk Jake trying to out talk Reverend Sam, the moderator? He preached on and on as much as when he comes over here of a Sunday afternoon."

Gladys said, "Wasn't that something when Reverend Sam got between Jake and Ollie? He stood on the podium!"

"That's more than Ollie and Jake stand on," Narcissa said.

"For sure, Jake wasn't free and easy with straight talk," Mabel lectured.

"That's because he's a farmer," Gladys said. "Farmers who talk on themselves never talk straight."

Mabel wore a mischievous grin. "Their debate was like a vacuum because it pumped out a lot of thoughtless air."

Gladys wanted to keep to the topic. "What's the critical difference between Ollie's and Jake's positions?"

Narcissa beat Mabel to an answer. "The critical difference was you could see Ollie's head above his podium, only Jake's ears to the sides of his."

Floyd said, "Sure am glad Jake hung picture posters on the walls or you wouldn't have seen anything of him but those ears."

"Jake looks so poorly on his posters," Narcissa said, "if he'd just walked off the road into the nursing home, nurses would have rush him off to emergency."

"Thinking on summing up, Ollie's wasn't hard to understand," Mabel said, "if you put in the verbs."

Floyd had his own thought. "Jake's voice had more to it. His sinuses exploded all over."

"The debate was nothing but opinions," Gladys said.

Mabel answered. "You're right, Gladys. Nothing was said about the duties of the Trustee because I believe they know so little about fighting fires, handling poor relief or library books."

Floyd wondered, "Fighting fires? Jake? He's a three cup, three donut man down to the town café, never been a volunteer fireman."

"Then why is he running?" Narcissa asked.

Gladys commented,. "To convince his insurance agent a deer lit the fire to his barn."

Mabel said, "Ollie's reason for running must be to upgrade his yard. He wants to control the old fire trucks. Last time my grandson took me for a ride, Ollie's place had nothing but washing machines, dryers, and lawn mowers rusting around his repair shop. An old pumper would be an upgrade."

Noticing the gathering of wheelchairs and ambulating residents at the door, Gladys said, "As for me, I'm asking head nurse Alice to be in my room when I vote my absentee ballot."

Mabel agreed. "Yes! Just in case a political hack brings it. They can't be allowed to slicker any resident!"

"Right on," Floyd said.

Narcissa asked, "What does 'right on' mean, Floyd?"

"I don't rightly recollect," he said. "I heard them TV Hip Hop fellows say it."

Residents pushed open the activities door to get favored places for bingo.

"Meeting adjourned," Gladys said. "Grab your places for bingo."

Grandpa took his leave.

DEXTER'S BARBERSHOP

Dexter, the barber over to west Union Township, was right tall for a barber, eyes so high his view was pates with hairless circles from half dollar size to coconut smooth. Knees playing out, Dexter usually turned to stool sitting to roll around the barber chair, scissors nipping away wild growth off back acre farmers and Grandpa. Dexter was truly appreciated by the good old boys, not just because he was the only barber in a twelve mile circle, or because he trimmed ear hairs to restore hearing or eyebrows as neat as Schilkelgruber's moustache, but because he listened, many approving nods and grunts made to bull tossers.

Dexter weren't often on Grandpa's mind, (or was little else), 'cept when his head's dangling side hairs picked up dust balls getting slippers from under the bed. Time for a hair cut, his hair as long as Grandma's; he needed a pruning to tell the difference between them.

Over to Dexter's, Grandpa expected to hear farmers spouting on their yields per acre, or brooding sows, or calves ready to give up livers. No one in line, Grandpa climbed right up and sat down in the old fashion chair. Dexter tossed cloth, like them Toreadors down in Mexico did for bull fighting. It wrapped around Grandpa's scrawny neck. No sooner fastened with a clothes pin, than Dexter took to clipping hairs still clinging to head bone. Nary a word spoken! Talking came when the little hair left was combed and Dexter wanted $8.

Buzzing of the clippers was overpowered when Orville, beard down to bib overall pockets, walked in, lips flapping like that all mouth, no brain Republican radio broadcaster. Orville was steamed over a run in he had with Tillie who lived the north side of the closed toxic waste dump. He described her as an old heifer, barely this side of human evolution. Right up in his face she was, and chastised him for taking Melvin's side over Freida's mouthing off.

"He be my boy Gordy's best friend," Orville told Dexter, "and I stick by Gordy's friend, no matter."

Grandpa, listening in, wondered on the meaning behind 'no matter.'

Orville quickly satisfied the wonderment. "Big Tillie said Freida said Melvin's a sissy boy. So why he be visiting Freida down by the pond, if he be?"

"He be!" Tillie yelled across the shop, the front door riding her rump to close. "Melvin should have his name on the list city cops make out on them that don't do right by nature."

Grandpa sensed Dexter's clipper picking up steam when Tillie walked right over to Orville's place on the side bench and ballooned over him. Grandpa wasn't sure Orville wasn't on to hitting a woman, assuming Tillie was female, but he was on to getting right up in her face.

He said, "Melvin ain't a sissy boy. If he be a sissy, why he be over to Freida's place by the pond?. Melvin ain't fishing for no carp. Why you say what you say, Tillie?"

When Dexter's scissors got frantic working on Grandpa's ear hairs, he held his head as still as a brick in a house wall.

Tillie got right down to it. "Freida done told me Melvin be a 'sissy'. She went to high school with him. She was a cheerleader and he was on the track team, ran the dash. She said Melvin's shorts puckered like all boys running dashes. She said weren't no jockstrap bulking up his runner's shorts, it were his Grandma's panties."

"His Grandma's?" Orville took a breath of air, and said, "Freida said she knew that way back then? Don't believe it. I stick by my boy's best friend, no matter. Them boys was just advertising for cheerleaders."

Tillie said, "For cheerleaders? Ha! Freida says all them track runners were sissy boys."

"Not the long distance runners!" Dexter hollered to be heard over to the town tavern.

His legendary traits of calmness and quiet were dropped like Grandpa's hairs, who was praying the razor on his neck wasn't a guillotine.

Orville's and Tillie's eyes rolled like stripes on the barber pole.

Dexter let them know the truth of it. "I was the team's only runner to make State. Ain't you ever wondered why Melvin, not me, got a track scholarship to Back State Junior College when Coach took to coaching track there?"

"Tillie's full face done puffed up. "Didn't Gordy go to Back State, Orville?"

"Dang," Orville said as he churned out the

barbershop door, beard and words drifting behind him. "Melvin be coming over to my place to stay with Gordy!"

INHERIT: DOWN, UP OR OVER?

"None of them kids made a will," dairy farmer Hezikiah said coming up the steps to rest a while with Grandpa on his front porch. Homer, the Hired man was a step behind Hezikiah, his usual way. Both plopped down to their comfort.

"Don't know," Hezikiah continued, "if the property left is going down to the child, up to the grand folks, or over to the brothers and sisters no matter most of them is in jail."

"Who you talking of?" Grandpa said, taking his comfort on the red wood chair.

"Ferd and Ethel Burrow and Charley and Mytle Pike."

"What about them?"

"You didn't hear! Ferd and Ethel done run into a deer that came through the pickup's window. Not rightly sure if the deer killed them or the crash. Either way, dead. Same day, Charley fell into the drain pond when he heard the news. Mytle reached for him, slipped in too. Both drowned. Sad! Their folks be fighting over what's left behind."

"Over little Oscar?" Homer said.

"More than Oscar, but he be the center of it being the sole survivor and Ferd and Charley were doing right good at farming. You see, the word over to the township café was Ferd Burrow got Mytle Sky in the family way and

73

wouldn't marry her. Said it wasn't his. She went on to have baby Oscar and adopted him out to Charley and Ethel Pike. Ethel be one of the Meadow tribe. She and Charley raised pigs over to the south east of the township. Must of something happen after that there adoption, 'cause Ethel took off carrying little Oscar along to move in with Ferd on his grain farm just north of Charley's place. When Charley got the divorce, out to spite Ethel, he married Mytle Sky; and then didn't Ethel turned right around and marry Ferd Burrow."

"Just a minute," Grandpa said. "Ferd, who claimed he wasn't the father of Oscar, married Ethel, Oscar's adoptive mother? And Mytle, the natural mother of Oscar, married Charley, the adoptive father?"

"That' the way of it," Hezikiah said. "Ferd claimed he weren't the real father, though Mytle claimed he was. Anyhow, when Ferd and Ethel hooked up, Ferd was Oscar's stepfather. Ethel still the adoptive mother. Charley, the adoptive father, never did have the court cut that legal tie to Oscar when he divorced Ethel, or when he married Mytle."

"Who do Oscar belong to?" Homer asked.

"Ethel was raising him," Hezikiah said. "Now her folks, Hal and Tessie Meadow have Oscar, though Mytle's folks, Dale and Ginger Sky want him. That ain't the end of it. Darwin and Lucy Pike put in their claim too. All say Oscar's their rightful grandson. Not Henry and Lucy Burrow. Their son Ferd denied being the father. So do they. They want Ferd's property to come up to them or over to

Ferd's brothers and sisters. Being there weren't no Will on Oscar, them four families, Burrow, Sky, Pike and Meadow are fighting it out in Probate Court, sure enough, before old Judge Forum. He ain't know for making quick decisions. Oscar's going be in high school before the Judge comes around to it."

"There being no Wills," Grandpa said, "wouldn't Oscar take from Ethel, no matter she married Ferd, and from Charley, no matter he married Mytle? You said Charley never set aside being Oscar's adoptive father. Seems Ethel's property and Charley's will go down to Oscar."

"Maybe that's why all them grand folks got themselves Lawyers," Hezikiah said. "If one of them gets custody of Oscar away from the Meadow grand folks, they be in charge of what's rightfully coming down to the boy. About Ferd's property, Mytle's folks, Dale and Ginger Sky say a DNA test done proved little Oscar is Ferd's true son, so they not only want their daughter's boy with them but Ferd's property to come on down to the boy, not up to the Burrow folks. Henry and Lena don't take kindly to that notion. They say if Ferd fathered Oscar like them scientists hired by the Sky's say, Oscar is their blood kin and belongs with them over any grandparents with just adoption on the score card, or a mother who put Oscar out for adoption."

"Rather angry and tangled," Grandpa said. "A natural father, a natural mother, adoptive parents who divorced and remarried to the natural father and the natural mother, all of whom died on the same day leaving behind a child and two farmsteads. Four sets of grandparents, either by adoption or by blood who want Oscar and what's his."

"What be his?" Homer saked.

"Can't figure it," Hezikiah said. "How about you, Grandpa?"

"No one," Grandpa said, "denies Oscar was legally adopted when his adoptive parents died, though they were divorced and remarried, apparently to Oscar's natural parents. There were no other children born to either remarriage. Oscar is the only descendant. Seems whatever was left by the adoptive parents goes down to Oscar. The question to be answered, is: does the rights his natural parents go down to him? When Oscar was adopted, Mytle Sky gave up her rights to him. Ferd Burrow's rights were never established."

"That's it?" Hezikiah said. "Oscar gets from Charley Pike and Ethel. Who gets Ferd's place if Ethel's name not on the deed."

Granpa answered, "That's why it'll take Judge Forum a while to come down with a ruling."

"Seems to me," Homer said, "it be good to write down how you want your stuff to go, be it down, up or over. Going to town to see Murl, the lawyer."

LILA'S CAFÉ

Conversation at Lila's Café was the main source of updates on Union Township folks and their doings: past, present and future.

The Breakfast Special, three eggs over easy, sausage, fried potatoes and toast of home made bread was reason enough for Grandpa and Grandma to drop in for breakfast of a morning.

There were additional benefits. Grandpa never tired looking over the history of the town displayed via photos hung on the walls, while Grandma took kindly to being updated on the well being of folks from the area.

While waiting on waitress Minerva to bring the orders, Grandma was a bit disconcerted none of the lady regulars were around to chat. The only regulars present were the sewer pipe crew up at the counter.

Grandpa, sipping hot coffee, took to looking over class photos of Union Township's high school graduates. "Look Babe, there's young Noah," he said, "in the class of 1955. How full his face was. Same smile as now. Look at all the hair. I wondered if he borrowed that suit. I bet that was the last time he wore a shirt and tie. They don't go well with a grain farmer's bib overalls. Red bandanas do."

Grandma pointed to a photo of a basketball team.

"The 1955 team," he said. "That big smile had to be on Noah. Look at his uniform. It fitted like a bathing suit. He isn't but five foot eight in today's work boots. If all the other guys weren't sitting, that was one short team!"

"Over there, 1953, is that our neighbor?" Grandma said.

"It has to be," Grandpa said. "Hezikiah looks as worn out in that old photo as he does now a days out to his farm. There he is again, the photo on the wall to your left. It says it was taken in 1950. Look at the glow on his face standing beside his champion Holstein. The caption reads he, his cow that is, had won the 4-H prize for a supreme brand of milk at the county fair."

"I can see yesterday's boys in today's men, Noah and Hezikiah," Grandma said. "Hair fringes are a lot less now than the crops they grew back in their youth."

"Isn't that the way of us aging males?" Grandpa said. "If it wasn't for ear and nose hairs, we'd be mistaken for billiard balls! You, babe, have a head of grey hair fuller and rounder than an alabaster Afro. I never lose sight of you when we're walking different aisles in big box stores."

She ignored the jibe. "When did Homer graduate?" She asked.

"Let's see if I can find it. Homer's class would have been about fifteen years later than Hezikiah's," He scanned the class pictures. "No Homer in the class of 1968, or five years before, or five years later." About to give up, he said, "Hold on! Is that turkey holding a boy, or was it the other way around. Homer? If it is, he looked about ten. The caption reads, 'Grand Champion. Sold for $40.00. Probably for some restaurant's thanksgiving banquet. No name of the boy."

Lila's Special before him, a glance up from his eggs, Grandpa could tell Grandma had gone into her eavesdropping mode, a CIA operative seeking details. It was amazing the way she never missed a bite while radar ears scanned the café's conversationalists. She wasn't a busybody. Whatever was overheard was kept quiet, except, from time to time, she's tell Grandpa. With his aging memory, it quickly sunk to the bottom of his brain.

She said, "I hear them talking about impostors; the boys on the sewer pipe crew and Minerva, the waitress."

"Impostors? What impostors?"

Grandma didn't offer an answer. He knew her hearing was better than a bat's. His, on the other hand, never heard much unless the sound was louder than the ringing in his ears. Her voice was. A Hoosier twang gave her words a pitch higher than his ear ringing.

"Now there's talk of a Grand Jury," she said.

Grandpa hunched shoulders as if he said 'so what'. Nothing to do with a Grand Jury was of interest, as long as he hadn't been subpoenaed to testify.

Grandma raised a finger, a signal her antenna had detected more intelligence. "They're saying the Grand Jury is getting after a Hector Koff for using impostors to take medical exams."

Finger down, Grandpa nodded and took a bite of sausage. He thought he'd better get to eating faster if she were honed into targets.

Finger up. Grandma let out a stream of words. "Minerva said, 'My best girlfriend Lana's ex-boy friend

Freddy got HIV, not from Lana, she's clean.' Minerva said, 'Freddy's folks were poor as Pastor Millstone. No health insurance. Then Hector Koff, the life insurance man, came on to them.' Minerva said, 'Freddy was bad off, so Hector said buy life insurance on Freddy. His brother Larry could take the medical and give the blood sample. It worked."

Grandma shook her head. "Those sewer crew boys think Hector's a hero."

Finger down. Grandpa dipped a piece of toast into the third egg.

Finger up, Grandma whispered, "the greasy guy over by the sewer pipe crew said 'Hector got Ada to take out a policy in the name of her sister Bernice who is sick as a dying dog. Ada did the medical and their ailing Ma gets the cash when Bernice passes."

"A triple play," Grandpa said. "Bernice through Ma to Ada.

Counter conversation cooled when Noah, Hezikiah and Homer, the hired man, entered the café and headed over to join the Gramps.

Minerva left her sewer pipe crew, retrieved a pot of hot coffee and came on over to fill five cups. She took three orders of Lila's Special, then said, "Noah, I heard the Grand Jury done come down on Hector Koff."

"Hector? My nephew?"

"That's right." Before she left to order up, she said, "They're getting him for using impostors to take medical exams and physicals for real sick folks what apply for life insurance. The boys up at the counter think right good about Hector."

Noah's eyes followed her as she walked to the kitchen, then he groaned. It came to him every body in the café had the word long before him out to southwest Union Township. He said, "Hector sold me a policy."

"Did you take the physical?" Hezikiah said.

"I don't recollect I did."

Homer the hired man hadn't an awareness of Noah's anxiety. "I didn't need no impostor to pass that there test."

"You sure could have used one to get out of grade school," Hezikiah said to shut him up.

There was uneasiness all over Noah's face when he again said, "I didn't have no physical."

"Maybe Hector had your medical records, seeing as you are kin." Hezikiah said.

"If he had my medical records, he needed more," Noah said without haste.

"How much life insurance did you buy, Noah?" Hezikiah said.

"$50,000."

"Whose the beneficiary?"

"Seeing I'm a widower with no kids, my only sister, Nellie."

"Isn't Nellie Hector's Ma?"

"Dang," Noah said. "Nellie's in a bad way, worse than me, and Hector is her only kid."

"When did you get the policy?"

"About two years back."

"More than two years?"

"What difference does that make, if Hector sold me a policy on the wrong," Noah said.

Hezikiah said, "Most life policies say if two years go by and if you're still above ground, the insurance company can't come after your beneficiary after you ain't around, that being Nellie, or maybe Hector. Company had two years to have checked it out."

"Hector!" Noah said. Reflection taken, he said, "that boy's too clever for his own good. Impostors, Grand Jury and all! How about Hector doing for others without putting out a dime!"

Vaunceel, the cook, came out of the kitchen, white apron spotted egg yoke yellow, and served three plates of the Special to the farmers.

He said, "Yours is on me, Noah. Hector done did right by me!"

BIG-DOUGH BENNY

Grandpa's volunteering for the nursing home ombudsman took on a real different chore when she asked him to call on Jupiter. The old black man was asleep in the bed north of a wheel chair. Was he? Grandpa saw nary a sign of visible breathing. Jupiter's mouth was as open as a hooked fish's. Expired? A cold breeze rustled the hairs on Grandpa's neck. Death of a man in a nursing home bed looked not at all like death remembered from the battlefield. There, Grandpa told it, 'screams pierced the thunder of incoming shells, heads rolled back as if disengaging from bodies as an orgy of blood re-colored fatigues'. Here the elder was silent, no reddish fluid, the head laid as if mounted on his pillow. No pulse?

"Lord have mercy on your soul, old fellow."

As Grandpa remembered it, a wide hand opened suddenly grasping his wrist. Brown wintry eyes glowed and lips moved, "I needs all the mercy the Lord can give."

Grandpa said he fought making noise, but a soft whinny sneaked out of his mouth. "Thought you'd gone to heaven," he said composing himself, the cold bony hand holding tightly.

"Needs to make amends first," wintery eyes' said. "You new?"

"A volunteer," he said, disguising choking up. "The ombudsman asked me to call on you. I thought you weren't doing well. I didn't mean to wake you."

"Don't needs no more sleep, man. I needs to get Big-dough Benny to call before I pass."

"Where does he work?" Grandpa said.

"Work? Big-dough ain't took to work. Old Herman worked life a laborer. It be hard work, hard money. Raised Benny Mack in the right. He don't want hard work. Big-dough's on the corner by Calvin's Place up in the big town. He deal dope. Dope-heads name him Big-dough."

"Benny Mack's your son?"

He let loose the wrist he squeezed. "Ain't no more Benny Mack." Tears puddled in the basins of his eyes. "Get Big-dough Benny to come on to visit before I pass. I be wanting to give him Mama's bible."

"I'll do everything I can, Mr. Mack."

As Grandpa told it, he was fascinated by the request for a visit, but he questioned whether he could bring it off. Any hope of getting to dope dealer Big-dough Benny at Calvin's Place in the big town had less a lesser chance for success than an Israeli getting a Hezbolah to visit a synagogue.

Grandpa wondered would Big-dough Benny be around in afternoon day light at Calvin's? That was one mean part of the big town for any man, much less an old one with light skin to safely cross a street, not to mention Calvin's place. There wasn't any doubt as to why the ombudsman sloughed this off on her only volunteer. No wonder she had but one volunteer! Still, it was a trip to help a resident carry out a last wish!

Parked at the curb, Grandpa looked out his pickup's

window over to Calvin's Place. He said he saw a tough looking quartet eclipsing the corner. When a wine-head staggered out and saw the toughs, he wasn't too far gone to walk the other way. Then an old man came from in front of the pickup to cross the street. He pushed his face up against the grimy window, but said nothing when a big muscled dude came out and led him by an arm through the parking lot to a cardboard box back by garbage cans.

A few vacant lots to Calvin's east was a Laundromat. Women in its front window sat as if in Holland, not selling themselves, just eye balling the passing parade. Children at play, some in coats, were outside running in the vacant lots playing tag, getting home free. Cars with folks who'd never lived in the neighborhood, gawked from behind locked doors, rolled up windows, cars in gear. Grandpa got out, locked the truck and crossed the street.

"Got a quarter, man?" a boy, not five, said. Big, brown eyes begged.

"Broke," he answered.

Grandpa had removed his valuables before driving up to the big town, except five bucks and his driver's license. It left him feeling he was unfairly indicting Calvin's neighborhood. Then again, he'd be unfair, but quiet about it. He walked with purpose toward the toughs. They turned to face him. He nodded, their scowling mouths mindful of a platoon of mortar tubes. He turned abruptly and entered Calvin's. There was a minimal moon inside. Eyes adjusting, he saw tall to small men perched on top of rotating stools. He felt a spotlighted leading man. The silence was intimidating. What were the odds of getting out of Calvin's a non-eunuch? Grandpa said he wasn't sure just how long he stood there feeling like a lone Elm surrounded by lumberjacks. As his eyes focused, the men at the bar didn't look too threatening. Some turned away, getting back to booze and chatter. The guys at the tables got back to their cards. He wasn't of much interest.

"I'm Calvin," the barkeep said. "This my place, man. Tell me what you be doing in Calvin's?" His tone was civil. His long upper body was within a cement colored solid twill shirt, no fat anywhere, with shoulders that must have excelled at football.

Grandpa said he felt comfortable enough to walk over and talk to the barkeep. "I'm a volunteer for old folks in a nursing home. I'm here hoping to get a message to the son of a very ill man in Union Township Nursing Home. I was told his son hangs out here."

Calvin's eyebrows lifted when he said, "How a black man get over to Union Township?"

"I don't know, but I know his son's name is Benny Mack. Do you know him?"

"Mack? Don't know nobody named Mack."

"He might be better known as Big-dough Benny."

Before Calvin answered, a chair crashed. Grandpa said he turned and caught a little guy's burning stare. He looked ready to sail some where, dressed fit to walk Fifth Avenue. He had his right hand in his pocket.

Grandpa admitted to gulping, seeing as he had

memories of movie show Western shoot-outs. He raised his arms slowly. Bar stool sitters dispersed.

"Don't do no bad in my place Big-dough," Calvin said forcefully. "Out side!"

Oh Lord, Grandpa thought, Calvin cared only about not messing up his place.

"Why you want with me," Big-dough Benny said, hissing.

"I'm here at the request of your father in Union Township Nursing Home. He's not doing well. He wants to see you. Wants to make amends. Asked me to look you up to tell you."

"You dumb, you think I believe that."

"I am dumb for coming to tell you your father wants to make amends. He said he wants to give you Mama's bible."

"Mama's bible?" Big-dough Benny's mouth twisted in surprise. He looked to Calvin, who nodded positively.

Grandpa remembered Calvin's friendly nod clearly because Big-dough Benny took his hand out of the bulgy pocket. Was he grimacing? Smiling? It was difficult to tell with the light reflecting off his gold front teeth.

"Mama's bible?' he said, rolling his head. "Old Pop say he be giving me Mama's bible? They put me down in Mama's bible." There was joy in his sound. "You for real, man!"

"Not for much longer at this pace," Grandpa said, his hands cupping his heart. "Union Township Nursing Home's visiting hours are from 8:00 AM to 8:00 PM every day. Here's one of the ombudsman's brochures. On it, I've written my name and phone number. If you need me to work out details, just leave a message. Nice to have met you, Big-dough, and you too Calvin."

"You don't mean it," Calvin said.

With relief, Grandpa tilted his head and twisted his lips with a skewed smile. He was about to get his butt out of there and into the pickup when Big-dough Benny said, "Hold on, man. Take me out to old Pop."

As that was what Grandpa had come for, he would. He led the small swell to the pickup. Its sight caused Big-dough to choke up, eyes golden as his front teeth.

"Oh man! I got on my houndstooth. Ain't you got decent wheels, man?" He looked in. "It be clean?"

"It is. Can't do more than the speed limit either, so no cops."

They got in, the motor kicking over like a toddler against bed slats. It stuttered but took off, a back fire the ultimate distress to the finely fashioned passenger. He remained silent the distance to the nursing home. Grandpa pointed it out.

Big-dough's first look shocked him. "Man, you took me back at Boys Reform School." He looked about to satisfy his whereabouts. "Man, I know we not be down state but how could they moved the reform school way up here? Old Pop doing time in there? Me and Old Pop ain't never hit it off, but Old Pop don't deserve finishing off a hard life in a place like Boys Reform School. Old Pop worked honest all his years. This all he dot to show for it?

That be wrong, man."

Grandpa said Big-dough Benny must have felt something he'd not felt before: shame.

When they entered, out of their sight in the front room, a woman, Stuffed Olive it turned out, hollered "rapist!"

"What the!" Big-dough Benny said, jumping a foot in the air. Back on tile, he saw her come of the stuffed couch and take off racing down the corridor, turning sharply to the right. He hadn't seen a faster runner since his last track meet.

Before Grandpa could explain Stuffed Olive meant the 'rapist' was him, a second later a very round nurse came down the hall waddling toward them like a gun boat.

"Can I help you," she said, her eyes giving him a fishy look, totally ignoring Grandpa.

"I be here to see Old Pop, Herman Mack," he said.

"Herman? He's your father?" she said, doubting the little runt had one. When she noticed Grandpa, she left, hips like firing pistons.

"Oh man," Big-dough said.

Grandpa felt for him. The scorn of the wide-load woman had poured like water.

Big-dough Benny said, "she ain't got nothing on my reform school teachers. Even coach dissed me. He saw nothing but a scrawny circus freak with a crooked back and bowed legs, no matter I be the fastest in the dashes. Big-dough could buy this place and Boy's reform school from a day's cash. He flipped through a wad of dollar bills.

Impressed at the size of the wad, not Big-dough Benny, Grandpa led him to Herman Mack's room. "I'll wait out here," he said.

"Stay near the door, man. No telling what Old Pop's up too."

Big-dough Benny saw the back of his father's head, a lot of hair, white as wool. He spoke softly, "Pop? It's Benny."

"Who you say?" Mack turned to see. "Benny? You not in jail?"

"Ain't never been in jail, Pop." The broad face the son knew for its glaring stares, the hands large as horse hooves that shook his body, weren't more now than a Halloween skeleton's, but the eyes had fire.

"You did time!" he said, his sound curt, cutting.

"Juvenile time, Pop, not big time." He remained calm.

"They going catch you, Benny." It was said with hopelessness.

"Pop, I ain't here on that," he said, losing patience. "I here to get Mama's bible like you told the old white man."

"He done told you that?" He said it to jibe.

"Don't diss me, old man." Big-dough Benny had already had enough. "That old white fool put his nose on the line coming to Calvin's just to tell Pop say come and get Mama's bible. Could have waited 'til you passed."

"Wouldn't have missed you," Mack said, hissing 'missed.'

90

"I be going."

Mack raised his fist in Benny's face. "Going whop you first," he said.

"Going what?" Big-dough Benny said, astonished the sickly old goat had energy enough to double his fist. "Never could catch me, Pop!"

"You was fast," he said. He looked at his son a moment and surprised himself by smiling. "Near as fast as Jesse Owens!"

"Near as fast? Jesse see nothing but my butt, elbows and heels he run against me!"

Old Pop, for a dying man, laughed fit as a healthy hyena. Big-dough Benny chirped like a sparrow, triggering Old Pop to hilarity, igniting Big-dough Benny to elation.

Neither could explain which one first cradled the other, but neither was going to be first to let go.

COOTIE HUNT

Homer, the hired man, and his companion, Hired Dog, seeing Grandpa lounging on his front porch, saw fit to pull their pickup over onto the gravel driveway to stop and visit. It was a good day for visiting, being a comfortable Sunday morning after chores and Hezikiah and his Missus away churching. No sooner were welcomes tossed, than Hired Dog jumped up on the pillows of a wicker chair and took to scratching himself from ears to where ever he itched and his hind legs could warp to claw.

Grandpa took note. "Fleas?"

"Cooties," Homer said.

"Cooties? I haven't heard 'cooties' since Korea," Grandpa said. "Whether cooties, fleas, tics or lice, Grandma isn't going to take kindly the dog is scattering them all over her furniture."

"Get down, dog," Homer commanded. "Sit."

Mournful eyes pleaded, but the critter obeyed, a look of annoyance freely tossed.

Comfortable in a lounge chair, Homer said, "What about that there Korea, Grandpa? You get cooties over there?"

"Cooties! We did all we could to avoid them. Up on the front line, after we dug fighting bunkers, we dug communication trenches to connect the bunkers, then 'commo' trenches back to the rear slope. Like working on the farm, soldiers had chores, too. I can still hear Sergeant

Warren yelling while going from bunker to bunker, 'Cootie hunt on the back slope.'"

Homer and Hired Dog relaxed. They were up to hearing a good story.

Grandpa said, "all but the three left on guard duty took Sarge up on it. Hunting for lice was a break from front line routine. In addition to looking for them bedded down in fatigues, GIs shot the breeze and rested sore backs and hands from digging trenches. My squad leader, Sarge, hated lice. He said old soldiers back home in Iowa called them cooties during the first world war, but had to live with them in the trenches. They didn't have modern cootie powder then. In Korea, we GIs hunted and destroyed them, then powdered seams even without sight of a critter, especially making Private Diemer dust himself near ghostly. He ferried a boat load of cooties and remained the headwater of his bunker buddies."

"As I remember it, I was first up the communication trench to the reverse slope and found an ammo box to sit on. I took off my fatigue shirt to check seams for lice but found none. Sarge and the others came up trench removing their shirts. They spread out, sitting on rocks and ammo boxes to start searches. Next, I took off my undershirt to check it out but the evening air was so chilly from the wind off the north mountains my freckles blanched. I looked a TB consumptive but found no cooties. As the wind was too biting to sit long without it, I pulled it back on."

"'Don't you have lice, Red?' Private LaSapio asked me.

"'No! I don't know why, maybe my Celtic ancestors passed on some kind of immunity.'"

"LaSapio had a wide eyed look. 'Immune, I'm not, being as Deimer's in my gun hole,' he said holding his shirt while his fingernails bisected the caught culprits. 'Got more powder, Sarge?'"

"There was already so much louse powder around his undershirt, LaSapio looked a swan."

"'Here's another packet.' Sarge said. He handed it over."

"LaSapio opened it and slapped himself all around. A cloud of floury white spluttered like a mist in a lowland. He sighed in exasperation and said, 'I forgot toilet paper. Be right back.' Stepping out of the mist, he pulled on his fatigue shirt. It waved behind him as he jogged up slope into the trench. Quickly down to the gun bunker and back, his shirt re-buttoned and toilet paper in hand, he ventured fifty feet down slope to drop a note of welcome within the new straddle crapper. Though privacy was afforded by a shelter half on either side, he was in view when he assumed the position. Just then something sounded like a Chink concussion grenade exploding about fifteen yards down slope from the slit trench."

"He leapt from the straddle crapper as if pole vaulting. When he landed, his feet hung up in his trousers. He somersaulted and rolled like a log, gravity having him by the butt. He chuted off the hillside disappearing from view."

"I took off after him. Others too. We saw LaSapio

below a rock overhang wrapped in a bush, face as purple as the distant mountains. When we reached him, his shirt and undershirt had been torn away."

"I yelled for Doc," Sarge said.

"Our squad's medic, Corporal 'Doc' Davidson came down hill fast as LaSapio had flown. Doc examined the unconscious guy's arms, legs, ribs. He felt for his pulse, and said, 'nothing seems broken but what's this around his neck?'"

"'I'll be!' Sarge said. 'A necklace? He's wearing a necklace. Wasn't when delousing. Must have put it on when he went back for toilet paper.'"

"Sarge moved the necklace over LaSapio's head to check it out. He said, 'it looks and smells like garlic. Why would he wear a ring of garlic around his neck?'"

"I said, 'LaSapio's Italian. Maybe his Roman soldier ancestors used it as an insecticide.'"

"'Insecticide!' said Sarge. 'Well, whatever.' He returned the ring of garlic to LaSapio's neck. 'Red, give me and Doc a hand to carry him up to Doc's bunker.'"

"We got him up slope, into the bunker and on Doc's bunk, the springs made of commo wire strung from barbed wire poles, the mattress C-ration cardboard boxes covered by a GI blanket. When LaSapio came to, he felt arms, legs, every where that hurt, most every part. Satisfied he was intact, he kissed the ring of garlic. I guess because he wasn't in Diemer's bunker."

Homer's head went to shaking like a branch in the

wind. A stare given Hired Dog, he said, "Grandpa, where can I get me a ring of garlic for dog's neck."

A shivered look returned, Hired Dog figured Homer was the one who needed the ring of garlic.

LONG LEGGED RATS

Grandpa headed his pickup north on the State Road up toward Culver, alert to dodging Union Township's long legged rats the four miles the road ran east of the lake and the marching fields of the military school. No matter he'd gone that way more times than a Hezikiah cow voided weekly, it always felt like he was driving through an ambush gauntlet.

Ambush gauntlet? Sure enough, but not from young lads marching in close order drill with old M-1 rifles at shoulder arms, but from terrorists that farmer Hezikiah and Homer, his Hired Man, called long legged rats.

Right! Long legged rats, deer, acting like terrorists lurked in daily ambush the south to north four and a half mile length of the State Road.

Why am I going on about Grandpa and long legged rats along the State Road? Because Grandpa was bragging he and his pickup were immune to terrorist deer. Hezikiah and Homer, the Hired Man, didn't cotton to the mouth spouting. They argued long legged rats hadn't the sense of a suicide racoon crossing a road lighted by headlights. Deer, they warned Grandpa, hadn't anything ingrained in their brains, except rut heat.

Settlers, nigh on back a century and a half ago, put horses to plow and cultivated every foot of Union Township's flat land, (about 100 acres) and as many of the hill sides as could be tilled. But the woods were too thick to fully harvest. They covered thousands of acres. Good for lumber, shelter, fire wood, out buildings, out houses and deer meat. Venison pulled many a family through a hard winter. (There wasn't any other kind in the Township). Over the decades deer nearly played out, but beef, hogs, goats, sheep and chickens flourished .

The deep woods remained.

Along came State Government's Out Door hirelings, who, pushed by city folk hungry for deer antler trophies, set out rules for hunting in woods. On account most city hunters couldn't hit the hind side of a round barn, old soldiers running close order drill over to the military school posted 'no hunting' across their many acres of wooded land. So the long legged rats took advantage, multiplying, especially in the woods running the east side of the State Road where 'no hunting' was the sign of 'lake people' worrying on the Vice President's fall out.

Grandpa's first half mile north was usually an easy drive. There was a clear view, golf course on the west, grain fields on the east side of the State Road, until the left turn by a time-honored cemetery. A small herd of deer, heads bowed to read the engravings, stood in silent prayer, assuming they believed. Grandpa always recollected where there were deer to the right of his pickup, there would be deer to his left. He slowed. He hadn't a need to rouse the buck and his harem off to the left, but the pickup's muffler could be indifferent. One time it gurgled. Deer to the right leaped left. Deer to the left leaped right. Sense of honor high, pledged to only crash into high priced vehicles, the deer always spared the rusting hulk.

Next sharp turn was to the right. Landscaped woods lined the left of the State Road for the next mile, sheltering lake people and nibbling does from view of ordinary folks like Grandpa. He pivoted eyes right. The houses of ordinary folks sat off the road in that direction, spaced apart every two or three acres. Over to the rental, deer who visited when summer people put out feed, had returned for a family reunion, all brown as dried leaves.

Easing by, Grandpa moved down the road where the lake peoples' private golf course opened the view. To the right, cottages (if mansions costing a few million were cottages) hugged the State Road. If the road hadn't been built years back for ordinary Union Township's folks, now-a-day politicians down in the State House would make it a toll road. Grandpa saw deer way out on the eight fairway, a pitching iron from the green.

Going up hill at the three mile mark by the old apple orchard, Grandpa's pickup coughed and slowed. Its muffler cleared its throat, not at traumatized deer, but at sight of the frazzled flag limping on a lamp post. It made it up, then down and up again by the military boys' golf course.

That rusty hulk of pickup was comfortable maneuvering through the ambush gauntlet.

Early of a Church Sunday morning, Grandpa had out his good car, (it only had 190,000 miles), heading north on the State Road. Thinking on Hezikiah's and Hired Man's warning, 'careful' was Grandpa's middle name. It was the time of the year for the rut, sure enough, but also for legal hunting. Orange heads were out in force to take advantage of amorous bucks.

Deer herds were thick in early morning light and Grandpa was a study of alertness the caution he took going past 'time honored cemetery' and its herd chawing down on flowers decorating headstones. He gently made the right turn passing deer nibbling grasses inside lake peoples' screen of trees, and deer at the free feed house. He saw a foursome of deer teeing up on the fifth tee of the private golf course.

The car, like the pickup that occupied a side by side garage, slowed driving up hill by the three mile mark and the old apple orchard, Grandpa recollected the flapping flag. He'd never seen a deer up on top of the hill, most likely because there were many fancy cottages left. Across the State Road a four foot fence ran north several hundred yards.

Was that a second flapping flag or a white tail jumping the fence?

Before Grandpa could say, a bolt of a bang rammed his driver's side door. He hit the brakes and looked back to see a downed kamikaze buck.

It must have figured to give its all fighting a bigger buck over the doe jumping the fence!

As far as Grandpa knew, his car was neuter. Opening the door, he though on pulling the carcass off the State Road when it got up and limped away, wounded in action.

As Grandpa saw it, the good car, unlike the pickup, wasn't immune to terrorists.

ANCIENT SCRIBE

Grandpa was asked by Union Township nursing home's social worker, Tessie, to call on Fergus in room 2, second pod, seeing as Grandpa had lots of education and warm blood running up to his brain through veins not yet clogged. Tessie told it the old coot, not Grandpa, Fergus, at every meal spouted poetry at the drop of a crumb, or puffing up the doings of his Scot-Irish forebears. Folks chawing down at meals were fed up to their shamrocks with the old professor's show-boating.

He knocked on the opened door. "Mr. Orr, I'm the township's volunteer. May I come in?"

"Yes you may. Volunteer? I'd heard there was one called Grandpa," he said in a wavering bass voice. "Grandpa? You're nought but a youth, but call me Fergus."

"Most folks out to the township call me Grandpa, but 'Your Excellency' will do."

That got a smile cut with an axe above a protruding chin and a twig of a neck. Grandpa noted Fergus must have been bred before Cal Coolidge's time. The seated man had blue eyes that singed flesh but looked a mummy with wide shoulders wearing a horizontally striped green shirt. His face carried more wrinkles than the Mississippi River had tributaries. A head of white hair was thinner than Grandpa's overhang. Fergus' long legs were entrapped by golfer's red trousers; but every inch of the man's backbone was upright in a hardback chair. He looked a technicolor scribe in a monastery, his quill illuminating a parchment of the Holy Script.

The weight of age in his voice, Fergus said, "Tessie, our potato shaped social worker who's none too social tells me it's not only St. Patrick's Day, but you're sprung from Irish immigrants."

"My parents," he said. "When the British had enough of the Irish by 1922, and the North six counties opted out of the Free State, my Dad, from one of those six, County Antrim, had enough and emigrated. He met and married my mother, from County Sligo, in Chicago."

"You are pure Irish, then." Fergus said.

"Pure Celt," Grandpa said. "My ancestors long before my parents kept the Anglo-Saxon hordes out of the West of Britannia, as it was called around 405 AD, and in 1169, invaded Ireland. The eight hundred years since, Celts from Britannia and Celts from Erin intermarried. I'm a Celt, but one with strong Gaelic overtones."

Fergus let loose a laugh of enjoyment. "You're okay, Grandpa. My connection to Ireland only goes back to 1606, the plantation of King James I. My great grandfather Blaine was Scot-Irish and lived in Country Antrim too. He was numbered among the United Irishmen against the British in 1798 when Papists, like your ancestors, and my Presbyterian people got sick of the Viceroy and took up arms under M'Cracken. After they failed, Blaine got out of there, sailed to France and then America, working his way out to Union Township. The Indians were peaceful so he built a cabin, married, raised children and crops and bragged himself a reputation as an Irish soldier."

"How about that! Descendants from County Antrim men meeting in Union Township nursing home," Grandpa said. "What are the odds?" Thinking on things odd, he remembered social worker Tessie's request something be done about the professor's non-stop poetry spouting. "I hear you taught Poetry over in the County's Junior College?"

"Not poetry, Literature," Fergus said, "but I do like to recite to enlighten my mates at meals. Given the quality of the prepared food, if it is prepared, a little poetry adds taste."

"For instance?"

"Are you familiar with Edward Fitzgerald's translation of the 'Rubaiyat of Omar Khayyam.'" He didn't wait for a response. "'*Yesterday, this day's madness did prepare*,' and at meals, I do mean the cooked food."

"I have a copy," Grandpa said, "but remember just a few lines. '*Waste not your hour, nor in vain pursuit of this and that endeavor and dispute; Better be jocund.*'"

Fergus interrupted, "*...With the fruitful grape; Than sadden after none, or bitter fruit.*'" He glowed like a firefly. "I should have figured you for an imbiber."

Grandpa was caught up in the moment, not remembering the sequence of stanzas, but lines came to mind. "'*The moving finger writes; and, having writ; Moves on...*'"

"You are a learned man, 'Your Excellency', the first I've met since sentenced here," he said and continued,

"'...Nor all the piety and wit, Shall have it back to cancel half a line.'" The smile on his face was as bright as a full moon. "Sit down in my lounge chair."

"Thank you," Grandpa said. The antique chair swallowed him. He had to look up from what seemed a place on the floor, but was pleased with himself for remembering a line or two. But how to curb Fergus' meal time prattling of poetry?

"I'm delighted," Fergus said, "to see another American of Irish descent interested in poetry, even if only translated by an Irishman. You say your Celts came out of the West of Britannia? Was St. Patrick born there?"

"He was, and today is his day, which reminds me," Grandpa said, and at the same time having a flash of inspiration. "I'm scheduled to give a talk in the dining room on himself. Come along and I'll tell you all you'll ever need to know about the good man." Not wasting a moment, though it took considerable energy, Grandpa got up from the low down lounge chair to help Fergus out of his straight back into a wheel chair. Out to the dining room, and into the midst of the dozens gathered, he left Fergus at mid-room.

It crossed Grandpa's mind as he viewed the old folks, but for walking miles a day, he was one of them, and not the youngest. He hoped his feet, knees and hips held out another decade. If ever into a wheel chair, his old farm house out to the far south of Union Township wasn't built to favor such a possibility. The nursing home was.

"Hello folks," he said, "I hope you don't mind,

because your Council Executive Committee ran out of money to hire talent, they had to settle on Union Township's Walking geezer to tell you 'Who Was St. Patrick of Ireland'. This is March 17 after all."

There was mumbling about the date, some questioning where February went.

"The Saint's name at birth, around 387 AD, was Suceth. He was from the west of Britannia. That's what the Roman occupiers called the country back in the fourth and fifth centuries, way before Fergus was born. Maybe!" That got a laugh. "The west is now called Wales. Suceth's father was named Calpornius, his mother Concessa. The family lived at Bonnavem, in the Roman province called Britannia Prima. Their native language was Britannia Celtic, with Latin the language of the rulers. Sixteen years later Suchet was seized by Irish pirates, called Scoti. It was the Roman Military that gave the Irish the name 'Scoti.' Some say it meant 'rovers', others 'raiders'. Suceth might have been captured by himself, Ireland's Niall of the Nine Hostages. In any event the young lad was sold into slavery in the north of Ireland. For six years near Slemish Mountain, he herded sheep, cows and pigs, all the while learning the Gaelic language and local customs. At age twenty-two, asleep and dreaming, Angel Victorius appeared and encouraged him to escape by going south 200 miles where he'd find a ship of fugitives. He did and they sailed, making it to Brittany. The fugitives hadn't an idea where they were as they wandered around. But for Suceth's knowledge of pigs, they wouldn't have had anything to eat.

Finally coming to a town, Gauls took his presence wrongly and locked him up for a month. It must have been his knowledge of the Britannia Celtic language, not his Gaelic Celtic accent, that convinced the Gauls he wasn't a raider. Patrick ultimately found his way to Auxerre, where, under Germanus, he took up studying for the priesthood. It was his calling after all, seeing that his father was a deacon and his Grandpa a priest.

"Suchet was ordained a priest in 432 AD. That's when he got the name Patrick. Seeing that the Irish were all followers of the Druids who liked to worship under oak trees, Church leaders figured they needed salvation. Who better than Patrick? He was armed with religious education, knowledge of Irish customs and spoke the language. So Pope Celestine, knowing Bishop Paladius hadn't lasted a year at Leinster, Erin, and had died on his way home, made Patrick a Bishop, and sent the best hope the Church had to change the ways of the fighting Irish.

"Over in Ireland on the feast of Beltaine, May 1st, Patrick attracted the locals by lighting fires before they were lighted at Tara, the seat of High King Loeghaire. It was the High King's honor to light the first fire on Beltaine. Angry, he hopped in his chariot, followed by many dozens of his armed men in their chariots, to put out Patrick and his fire. Calamity befell the King and his troops.

"Later, a Druid took on the newcomer, challenging Patrick to make it snow. It was the 1st of May after all, so he declined. Not the Druid. He got it to snow clear up to mid wheel of the chariots. Big time snow! The Druid was a hit among Loeghaire's men. Patrick wasn't bedazzled. He said to the Druid, 'now melt it.' The Druid said, 'wait until tomorrow'. Then didn't Patrick do what preachers do? He waved his arms, and the snow melted, nearly drowning all present. High King Loeghaire took note of the new man, dropped his own Druid, and hopped on Patrick's chariot. So began the ministry of Patrick to the Irish."

Smiles abounded.

"No matter Patrick preached non-violence, words not in the Gaelic language, Clan wars roared on all the while the good man went about the green sod and knocked down stone idols."

Time for a pause. He then said, "As a member of the Rusty Pipes Singing Group, I've a song that tells the story of Clan wars."

A tenor, he sang 'The Minstrel Boy to the War is gone."

Tears bedimmed Fergus' eyes. Even the hard of hearing were moved, so clear were melody and words.

Now was the time Grandpa figured on. He said, "Fergus told me he was Scot-Irish. Not so! He's really all Irish." There were raising of eyebrows, Fergus' fist. "Back around the year 500 AD," Grandpa continued, "three brothers and their followers sailed from Carraig, a large rock on the east coast of the north of Ireland, across the sea to Alba. The names of the brothers were Fergus, Lorne and Aengus. As Scoti, Irish, they formed a clan and settled down in Alba. Carraig, the rock, is now called Carrickfergus. The clan settlement is called the Highlands and Alba is called Scotland."

Grandpa waited for the buzzing to quiet, wheelchairs to turn back around to face him. "In honor of Patrick and Irishman Fergus, I will, tonight, make available to all diners of Union Township nursing home, the recordings of Irishman James Galway, the world's top Flute player, that you may have the peace and quiet of his sweet music at meals."

"The applause was monumental, considering the impairment of most folks movements, Fergus, first among them.

Social worker Tessie was thrilled beyond belief.

VOTING OTHERWISE

After faces, hands and other parts of the three flustered men were warmed over the living room's fire place, they took to sitting down.

"Seems," Hezikiah said while sinking deeply onto the sofa, "when township folks got behind one of our own to run for state representative, even gave Leonard a few bucks for yard signs, you'd think he'd be voting the way we local folks think. He be knowing we ain't for no long lease on that there toll road across the state, but dang if he paid that any mind. My new calf could have knocked me over when I heard Leonard voted for the lease like that groundhog of a governor wanted. That's top down, not bottom up representing."

Homer, the Hired Man joined in. "Leonard's brother Lamont be like that. Just last weekend, over to the library, he ambled in"

"To get a book?" Hezikiah said with amazement.

"Naw, one of them videos," Homer said. "Some little girl got the one he wanted, about 'Revenge of something'. Lamont told the little girl he wanted it. She said no. He said she weren't fit to root with his hogs. Dog gone if the girl's Mama didn't slug Lamont like to put him down for the count." Homer smiled. "Best day ever over to the library."

"You were there to get a book?" Hezikiah said, as astonished.

"Naw," Homer said, "one of them videos. Anyhow, aint't no surprise to me Leonard turned on us when he got down state."

Hezikiah nodding head agreed. He said, "Leonard be doing less good than a heifer's void. He say he be representing, but he be voting for that there seventy-five year toll road lease, no matter we against it. Sure as short summers follow long winters, that there bantam governor put Leonard up to it, most likely promising pothole repair out to his pig farm."

"I don't understand," Grandpa said, "How, in the face of majority opposition, the state assembly or governor would go ahead and lease a key asset like the toll road. It pays for itself. If a private Company, on the other hand, can make a profit over seventy-five years by charging drivers higher tolls, why not the State?" Grandpa, too, went to head shaking. "If leasing state assets is the way of the future, there are several state operated colleges that could be leased with tuition increased to the level of private Colleges. Profitable! But a lease of the toll road for seventy-five years? Grandpa said. "I'm seventy-five. Over those years I've seen President Hoover; the Great Depression; President Roosevelt; World War II; President Truman; the Korean War; President Eisenhower; the Interstate highways; President Kennedy's assassination; President Johnson; the Vietnam War; President Nixon; Watergate; Vice president Agnew's resignation; Vice President Ford, President Ford after the resignation of President Nixon; President Carter, America's diplomats seized by Iran; President Reagan; Iran-Contra; President George H. W. Bush; the Gulf War; President Clinton; the Bosnian War, Impeachment; President George W. Bush; 9/11; the Afghanistan and Iraq Wars. If there were, or are, anyone with the foresight to foretell what was to have transpired over that time, or what will happen the next seventy-five, I've not heard of them. Yet our governor, whose length of office can only be two terms, and Leonard, are going for a seventy-five year lease."

"For dang sure," Hezikiah said. "Leonard was as deaf as he is dumb when we told him when the tolls go up, shipping to market be up, likely doubling every few months like diesel and gasolene already do. Leonard's sticking it to us little folks."

"It's probable," Grandpa said, "Leonard's flu shot didn't take, and once he got his seat at the state capital he was exposed. Bird-flu got him."

Homer, who sat the other side of the fire place, said, "Bird-flu?"

"In a manner of speaking," Grandpa said, adjusting the heat of the flames, then resuming the indentation in his easy chair. "We listened to Leonard and advised him where we stood on the issues. He agreed, and never mentioned a toll road lease. So we gave him our vote, a flu-shot, so to speak. Our flu-shot didn't prevent infection. At the capital, he doesn't have to pay for bacon and eggs or chicken wings at the café. While he's Law making, there's breakfasts or evening banquets every day honoring someone who did nothing or something that never amounted to anything.

There, he hangs around with the governor, legislators, big money donors, lobbyists with gifts. Leonard can eat his fill, drink until his eyeballs are drains, be enticed by very friendly folks. Among those chicken-liver givers, he was exposed to Bird flu. When the governor sprung the lease on the legislature, no matter we later told Leonard we were against it, he was already infected with self-importance Bird-flu, and stands where the governor does."

"Going to need to follow the money," Hezikiah said. "Them foreigners signing the 75 year lease of the toll road are putting up front 3.7 billion dollars to take over the operating. To make it back, it's going mean making top dollar, like from toilet paper at rest stops."

"Toilet paper?" Homer said. "Got to remember to bring mine."

"Still need a buck in the slot to open a stall to make a major move," Hezikiah said.

"Big town's newspaper wrote," Grandpa said, "the foreign investors expect to make a profit each of the 75 years from tolls and other income, enough, not only to cover the up front 3.7 billion, but all operating and other costs. About 300 million dollars annually, 3 billion every ten years. Multiplied the 3 billion by 7 decades, you get 21 billion dollars, not counting five years."

"If foreign investors can do that, why not the governor?" Homer said.

"The governor," Hezikiah said," and Leonard figured 3.7 billion in hand not from the taxpayer can be spent while they are in office. They'll look darn good."

"Like the Federal Government," Grandpa said. "Cut income taxes, borrow from foreign investors, spend and let the next administration worry about deficits."

Homer said, "Leonard might get away with it. He'd have flunked out senior year of high school with me if'en his old man hadn't been on the school board. Leonard ain't writing those letters I'm getting."

The governor's people and party bosses are," Hezikiah said. "They work them up about why they're doing the right thing for folks too dumb to know the right thing."

"On the national level," Grandpa said, "top of the pyramid are politicians and political parties financed by wealthy corporate insiders, big money contributors and mysterious organizations with funny names that buy TV slots. Money flows like water through a broken dyke. So will the 3.7 billion the next ten years. The following sixty-five years won't have any toll road income coming to the state's credit."

"How's Leonard going to slop his hogs then?" Homer said.

'Top-Down', Hezikiah said.

WHICH WAY TO...?

If you're driving Union Township back roads and come across an ambulating old man, that's Grandpa, one who walks road side out beyond the beyond. If you want directions because you're car hasn't one of those Global Positioning System devices that tells you where you are, it's safe to ask Grandpa. Now he can tell you where to go, directions, that is.

Grandpa knew where he was going to walk each day on the back roads. Because of it, he became Union Township's top back road walker and critter undertaker. Critter undertaker? He didn't operate a furry funeral parlor or a cremation emporium, but he was a litter bearer for animals struck by pickups and left behind as road carcass.

Why am I going on about carcass kindness? Because of Grandpa's memory. He could not only remember the critter causality list by day and by kind but where he buried the corpus delicti in the woods.

One exception to burial. Walking south he saw, sprawled across the road, a critter flatter and longer than a six foot two by four. It looked as if it had been skinned. Sure enough, it had. It was a fur stole, a mink, and nary a pickup in sight. He at first imagined some fancy woman had done a striptease there and dropped it to wind up her act. Well, she didn't, more's the pity. He did imagined some second story man, no, crooks out to the township were too lazy to climb to a second story, a one story man

115

had liberated the mink from a fancy house. He must have tossed the loot onto the bed of the truck, where, after he told his moll what he had for her, he expected to wind up the night. Fat chance!

Back to Grandpa's memory, good for critter recall, bad for road location. He hadn't a GPS when it came to names of roads out in Union Township, the country, or streets over in the big towns like Culver, Burr Oak or Hibbard. He remembered county roads from north to south were numbered from1 to 20. He knew county roads from the east to the west had alphabetical names.

Trouble was, from north to south, County politicians weren't satisfied with 1 Road, 2 Road, 3 Road and so on. They messed everything up, as they were elected to do, and named the next road after 1 Road, 1 B Road, sometimes a 'C' road, and so on up the numbers. How was an aging fellow going to know which road didn't have a twin 'B' or triplet 'C'. Same for alphabet roads. Never satisfied with but one 'P' Road, like Peach, they threw in Pear, Plum and, as far as Grandpa knew, Pumpkin. To top all, State politicians added their two cents worth, (no lobbyists involved), with roads numbered even and odd, like politicians think, mostly odd, but also ran rivers like down stream, every which way.

One day, didn't a nice old lady driving south stop and asked if she were headed to Culver. Nope. Grandpa got her turned around, sending her north to the end of SR 117, then left onto SR 17. Trouble was, he meant left on SR 10, not recalling SR 10 and SR 17 separated a mile to the east where they broke off side by side fondling.

When Grandpa realized his kind act had redirected a township stranger, he worried the lady might be wandering aimlessly around, passing farm after farm afraid to stop where big dogs lumbered around wood piles. He put it out of mind figuring if she ran out of gas, Deputy Duty would be on patrol.

Then didn't Grandpa tell the next seeker of directions the road sought, Euclid, if not way over to the east side of the county, it had to be in town. The man claimed it wasn't, as he'd written the phone directions down, and Euclid he claimed, ran west off SR 117.

"Not so," said Grandpa, "there are no alphabetic county roads running east to west in the township, unless the one you want is underwater. The lake's the other side of cottages along SR117. I suggest you go north to the end of this road, then west a mile to a four way stop sign,.Turn left, and in Culver, ask for Euclid Street."

When the fellow drove off, Grandpa noticed he had a Disabled Veteran's license plate. The thought of the old lady he'd misdirected yesterday crossed his mind. Was she still wandering the township? What if that were the lot of the DAV?

A Veteran himself, guilt, something Grandpa rarely encountered, bothered him. He hurried home, kicked over his pickup's motor, and hurried north retracing the directions given. Didn't his eyes water when he caught sight of a home made street sign on a tree by a gravel driveway that ran west a distance up to a lake side cottage?

No sign of the DAV.

Only one thing to do, find Deputy Duty. As usual, he was off the road in evergreen trees by the four way stop sign. It was a prime source of revenue. Pulling off the road, Grandpa, ambled over and told his tale of misdirection of the DAV, mum on yesterday's misdeed. No need to overload the Minion of the Law with facts.

"Not to worry, Grandpa," Duty said. "I was ticketing him until I saw his plates. I gave a warning, him being a DAV and lost. I set him right. So it was you who sent him wrong?"

When Duty reach over for something, likely a ticket book, Grandpa professed guilt wouldn't plague him again. "Be back in a second, Deputy," he said. Quickly he went over to got the mink stole from his truck. Back , he said, "Found this on the road, Deputy. A lost item. If it's not claimed by anyone in the time set out by Law, sell it."

"Why thank you," Duty said, but a glare followed. "Had to set straight an old lost lady yesterday. Then this here DAV. No more, Grandpa. There's a nuisance law on the books. I hate to do this, the mink and all." He handed Grandpa a folded paper.

He opened it. It wasn't a nuisance ticket! It was a map of the township!

Deputy Duty said, "Best carry it in your hip pocket when hustling them roads."

From then on, map at hip, not a flask, Grandpa could show lost travelers every road, street and critter crossing in Union Township.

DEPUTY DUTY'S IQ SQUAD

"You won't believe what I'm on to telling you, Grandpa," Noah, the grain farmer, said with gravity, "and it's just between you and me. Right? Right. Deputy Duty done set up a Home Front IQ Squad against terrorism!"

Noah was a right husky man, as many muscles on him turning earth driving a tractor as he had back in the old days behind a horse pulled plow. He was up to date on the doings of Union Township. Grandpa, on the other hand, wasn't, and he was still overcoming city softness by walking the back roads and chasing a little pill of a golf ball into the high weeds golfers called 'rough'. It surely was 'rough' on the old geezer swinging that sickle he called a 'club' through an unforgiving tangle. One good thing, though. Grandpa found more golf balls than he lost.

"It was the President,"Noah said, "the President of these United States who gave Deputy the idea to set up the IQ squad. When the President said Home Land Security needed local information banks that can tie up to the Federal Government, Deputy got right to it."

"Against terrorism in Union Township?" Grandpa was on to feeling faint over the thought someone had an inclination to bomb the town's water tower. He stuttered as the words flopped out, "what's an IQ Squad?"

"You sure are out of it, Grandpa," Noah said, "since you took up all that golf ball chasing. Knowing you be an old soldier who fought for our country, I figured to bring you up to date. Deputy's IQ Squad gathers intelligence to fight terrorists!"

"Local terrorists?"

"Right! Deputy's using counterspies," Noah said, "who connect up with biker gangs, anti-war protesters, greens, porno web surfers, meth makers, locals like that."

Grandpa swallowed so not to stutter again. "Counterspies to look for meth makers, I understand. Anything else he needs to know about bikers, protestors, greens, porno surfers, comes out at the café over coffee or beers at the tavern or in the bleachers at ball games, or at the soda fountain. He should just have a few more cups of coffee than usual, or join the boys for a beer, or attend sports, have a pineapple soda."

Noah shook his head. "Shouldn't said nothing about meth makers," he said. "Only State cops, Alky boys and the Sheriff's undercover guys are on to handling meth. Can't conjure why they bypass Deputy. He tickets 'no-seat-belts-on' more than all cops in the county."

"Whatever," Grandpa said. "Because Duty's cut out of meth undercover he's set up counterspies on local citizens?"

"Not about meth! Deputy doing what the President asked," Noah said. "Deputy said those cops ain't looking into locals who're thinking of acting wrong, like those who made those disgusting attachments to Hezikiah's plastic cow out front of his place, or blocking entry to the toxic waste dump. So it's up to Deputy to show the Feds he's uncovering terrorists on home ground. Maybe even prevent a bombing."

"Bombing! Of what?" Grandpa said.

"Well there's the Township veteran's club and the cemetery cannon, the town's sewage plant. Deputy's sure he can show he's doing the right thing, then the Feds will give him big time security clearance."

"Security clearance?" Grandpa felt a chill ride his spine.

Duty's targets could include an old goat with a red thatch inclined to bad mouth state and national politicians in the Union Township Weekly's Letters to the Editor; or the grey hair Grandma he married who lived with him the last half century. Could Duty see Grandma as a community activist for singing with a quartet entertaining old folks at nursing homes; singing with her church's choir; singing for the next county's chorus? Grandpa didn't want to consider what Duty might think about Grandma's borrowing romance books from two Libraries, or playing cards outside Union Township's boundary lines.

Grandpa said, "how's Duty going about counter terrorism?"

Noah smiled. "Deputy's clever. He goes about arresting 'no-seat-belt-on' types most days, brings in money to pay the cost of his secret staff, while he's got them working undercover on bikers, at meetings, the soda fountain, tavern and the café. Reports come in on what they hear, and Nellie, Deputy's old maid auntie, puts it in the computer database. Deputy bragged to me on auntie's database's rap sheets, reports from the field, that's what they call counterspies' stuff, Library checkouts, town and township public records. Deputy's looking to tie into one of those Homeland Security Fusion Centers to pool his information with big time IQ Squads. He's on terrorism like maggots on a rotting racoon."

Grandpa didn't know whether to cry or laugh. Duty was truly the county's top cop on ticketing 'no-seat-belt-on" drivers, but recognizing potential terrorists, analyzing reports?

"Noah," Grandpa said, "I appreciate being brought up to date on Duty's IQ Squad, but I have to ask, if all those TV programs about gathering evidence on terrorist is as complicated as shown, who trained him and his spies?"

"Good old country common sense," said Noah. "Deputy's people pass on the gab to Nellie, she puts in the database, and he looks it over of a day."

"Sure he does," Grandpa said. "Who are Deputy's common sense agents?"

"That's secret," Noah said, "but because it's you, an old soldier and all, I can tell you this much. If you see Homer, Hezikiah's hired man, riding his bike amongst them bikers, he's working undercover. So is Homer's Mama, Delicta."

"Homer and Delicta have motorcycles?" Grandpa asked.

"Bicycle. Homer's pedaling with bikers going around the lake."

"That's mostly old folks, mothers, fathers and kids," Grandpa said.

"Not Union Township folks, except summer on the lake. Need to know about them."

"And Delicta is on a bike?"

"Naw. Too old. She's working days on the counter at the café, after school at the soda fountain to keep on top of township chatter."

Grandpa wondered had the President and Homeland Security flown alert colors one time too many?

LESS CASH FOR MEDS?

Noah's jar was full of vitality and his palaver was in full swing. "Sure enough," he said while rotating from his left cheek to the more ample right one on the hard back chair, "over to the drug store and soda fountain I'm not now putting down the cold cash on medicines like I had to before government money made it one of them old folks' benefits, cutting the cost of drugs." His face was right pleased with what Washington, not what the first president had done, but what them politicians had done that he'd voted for back in Union Township.

Hezikiah, Homer the Hired man and Grandpa were a'listening. Hezikiah, who was settled down on the cushioned swing, went to head shaking 'no, no', stirring more breeze on Grandpa's front porch than the overhead fan, one that used to hang from a ceiling in the dining room of a closed big town department store. Grandpa and Hired Man appreciated the cooling, plopped as they were on chairs with cushions that warmed expanses. Hired Man's hound, Hired Dog, crawled closer to the screen door by the steps to enjoy the wafting air on a windless evening.

"Cutting costs of drugs?" Hezikiah asked.

"That's right. Government money cut my drug costs by paying a lot on them."

Hezikiah head shaking went from 'no, no' to 'yes, yes', but without spirit. "Government money do pay some drug cost for folks on Medicare who sign up for that there

Part-D, but those same folks have to pay monthly rent to some insurance company and toss in extra at the drug store, not counting a double pineapple soda. They be calling it co-pay when druggist Lavon fills a bottle with what the doctor wrote out."

"A lot less than what I used to pay," Noah said, taking a sip from his jar.

"You do pay less," Grandpa said, "until after $2250. Then you fall into the donut hole and pay full cost of your medicines until Part-D restarts at $3600. That's $1350 dollars out of your pocket, plus paying premiums and co-pay all the while you're in that hole. What's more, the hole widens each year and premiums and co-pay go up with inflation. About seven years down the road, that hole will be as wide as $5066. You pay for all your medicines then until Part-D restarts, unless you run out of money and need extra help."

"Donut hole?" Hired Man said. "Lavon left the soda fountain to work in Lucy's bakery?"

"Naw," Hezikiah said, slopping a bit of the beast out of his jar onto his bib overalls. He wiped it up with a flashing tongue before speaking. "That's what they be calling the hole old folks fall into because them politicians won't do for us what they got for themselves, no hole."

Hired Man's head was either heedfully shaking or chasing flies from hair grease.

"Government money can't never satisfy every need of us old codgers, being we far outnumber them politicians," Noah said, sharp looks given Hezikiah and

Grandpa.

"Government money for Part-D," Grandpa said, "is going to save us old people some money, but it's going to cost all taxpayers, young, middle aged and old to make up the difference between what we pay in and about 80 billion dollars paid out each of the next ten years."

"80 billion be a whole lot," Hired Man said snickering. "Hezikiah always be yelling at me to go easy on the tractor,'cause I be spending that much running it of a year."

"80 billion a year," Grandpa said, "is 800 billion dollars over ten years. It's costing all taxpayers that much to bring a lot of happiness to the makers of drugs and health insurers."

"How so?" Noah said.

"Well," Grandpa said, "the costs of Part-D drugs are negotiated, not by the administrators of Medicare who negotiated hospital and doctor costs that we now have, but by for-profit insurance companies with for-profit drug companies. Looking at the prices set out in the plans, costs of medicines are 40% to 80% higher than the cost the Veterans Administration negotiated on similar drugs for old soldiers. For sure, no insurance or drug company is going into any doughnut hole. Whatever insurance company you sign up with, you pay the drug price of the deal they negotiated with drug companies."

"Why ain't Medicare negotiating?" Hired Man asked.

"It's been forbidden by a majority vote of

politicians in Congress," Grandpa said. "There's government money to be paid out, and campaign funds to come back in to the politicians. Medicare can't make political contributions. Insurance and drug companies can."

"You're just agin this administration, Grandpa," Noah said.

"More than this administration, Noah," Grandpa said. "I'm against those politicians in Congress who pass laws with borrowed money to spend government dollars to benefit the people, and while they are at it, enrich their big time campaign donors. If Medicare could negotiate for all old folks, I've read in the Union Township Weekly there's a report in the Senate the 800 billion dollars over ten years to be spent could be cut by 370 billion, maybe more. That's one huge savings. It's not to be, so it's one huge pay out to insurance and drug companies, one massive lug on current and future taxpayers. The increasing National Debt has been forgotten."

"Who kept Medicare out of negotiating?" Noah asked.

Hezikiah answered. "You pulled the election lever for them that's called conservatives. They not be inclined to let Medicare folks do the bargaining. Them conservatives just like you, Noah, looking for deals, cuts on fertilizer, favors from Ag-Company on seed."

"Good folks," Noah said, "deal when we can."

"You don't deal on borrowed money with nothing to cover it in the future. There's deals of a different kind with them politicians," Hezikiah said. "Like Grandpa, I read the Union Township Weekly. It tell some of those elected politicians who done worked to pass Part-D and passed it, quit the government to go work for drug makers for big-big money!"

"That ain't good!" Hired Man said.

"It isn't," Grandpa said."The law should be amended to give Medicare the opportunity to negotiate, and us in Part-D the choice between Medicare's or an insurance company's plans. We shouldn't be forced to go with an insurance company, or get no coverage, and a cash penalty if we later change our minds. What's more, insurance companies can drop drugs from their plans at any time while a person is still on it, but that person can't change his plan but yearly. So the particular benefit in the plan signed up for may not be there the next year or the year after."

"Sure are a lot of plans to choose from, " Hezikiah said. "Last count, 42 were floating around Union Township."

"42!" Hired Man said. "How's Mama Delicta going know what suits her?"

"If Delicta gets as much insurance company slick mail as I get," Hezikiah answered, "she ain't going to know what suits her. Better call one them social workers from Elder Help to give her a talking on it."

"Sure will," Hired Man said.

"Hear tell, Hezikiah said, " drug prices are a lot lower up in Canada. Thinking on pulling my trailer up there and camping a spell."

"It's a great place to visit," Grandpa said, "and

prices are lower for the same drugs insurance company plans carry, but our politicians won't let Part-D pay for them. Moreover, U. S. Customs have been seizing imports from Canadian Pharmacies sent to folks stateside."

"They do?" Noah said. "Ain't that illegal without one of them search warrants?"

"It's hypocritical," Grandpa said. "The majority of prescription drugs used by Americans and sold in our pharmacies are not manufactured in the U. S., but in foreign countries. Just like our flu shots are manufactured overseas. It's less a question of Law than the power of drug companies over our government."

"Lavon down to the drug store will do you right on prices," Hired Man said. "He be telling Mama she can save a lot of cash if she get Doc to switch her drugs from the big name you see on the TV all the time, to them that be like aspirin."

"A generic," Grandpa said, "is less expensive than a brand named drug. But Lavon is doing more than just looking out for Delicta. His drug store gets higher profit margins on generics: 54% as against 11% for brand named drugs. He makes about $5 more filling a prescription with a generic."

"I'll be dag-gummed," Hired man said. "Lavon is in on it too?"

"He ain't no dummy," Hezikiah said.

"As good as Part-D looked before this here talking," Noah said, "danged if it don't do more for insurance and drug companies, even Lavon, than us enrolled folks."

"There's more," Grandpa said. "The Commissioner of the Federal Trade Commission says some drug companies have been dealing behind the scenes with makers of generic drugs. Brand drug patents run out in 20 years, so to keep up the higher prices us consumers pay, some drug companies have been paying a lot of cash to makers of generics to keep them out of production."

"That's hard to believe," Noah said.

"It's in the Courts," Grandpa said. "Drug companies want more than a cut of Part-D."

UNION TOWNSHIP WEEKLY
GERIATRIC FOLLIES

It wasn't long after Accountant Lotta took an oath to tell the truth before the Grand Jury that Deputy Billie Bob took away Union Township nursing home's administrator, Elmer. The word around the township was Elmer used Medicaid dollars not intended for personal using.

This reporter was in the nursing home on the eve of ghosts when folks gathered in the dining room to celebrate Elmer's departure. Grandpa, the volunteer, was a special guest. Why? For whistle-blowing on Elmer's two hundred acre land purchase and new barn for Arabians, not the two footed turban types out of the Middle East, but the four legged animal type. Grandpa told this reporter he couldn't help but notice, seeing as the essence of the Arabians next door to his old farm house was wafting his way, pushed by west winds. Down to the County records, Grandpa said he was flabbergasted to read Elmer's name on the land deed. The Elmer of Union Township nursing home? It was. The word down to town café was nursing home administrators, unlike Aides and nurses that give all that loving care to old folks, got the hogs' share of the home's income, but enough to buy land and Arabians? Grandpa talked on it to the ombudsman who talked on it to the State Auditor. It turned out Elmer was using Medicaid money intended for those living in Union Township's nursing home. So now, State Health was running the place.

Residents were ready for the Halloween party no matter the scandal. Facial expressions of the old folks, not to exclude nursing and other staff, ranged from sleepy to ecstatic. The room was crowded, residents in colorful shirts, skirts and trousers, nurses in white, Aide's in pink, cooks in blue and maintenance men in brown. A few of the oldest ladies wore dark dresses befitting the eve of all hallows. Residents sat on chairs, wheelchairs and geri-chairs. Maintenance staff unfolded chairs for family members while Aides served decaffeinated coffee, tea and low calorie, sugar-free tidbits to guests and live-ins.

Cut out witches and wizards on brooms and cows jumping the moon vied for wall space with goblins and pumpkins. There wasn't gender discrimination as to broom riders.

The curtain stirred. State Health Nurse Belinda, the acting administrator since the handcuffing of Elmer, came out between folds to face the audience. She looked comfortable in pleaded front wheat colored corduroy pants, and a blue shirt. As the curtain opened, she said, "Ladies and gentlemen, I'm delighted to be at Union Township Nursing Home and to honor Grandpa for tooting his horn. I also have the privilege of introducing tonight's program that features the 'Sorcerers' and the singing of the Goldentones." The good looking woman turned and pointed. "Here are the Sorcerers who will analyze current events. The Goldentones will soothe feelings with songs!"

There was applause, though many residents expected faces less fearful than those on stage. Five Sorcerers sat in a semi-circle of wheelchairs. Antlered plastic helmets rested on frosty heads. Animal masks covered faces. Multi-colored cloaks, richly patterned, covered frail bodies.

On stage, the Goldentones clustered like a bunch of grapes; five on stools around two in wheelchairs, all on a platform an inch above the level of the Sorcerers. The singers ran the decades from seven to half eight. Bodies manifested various physical lamentations, but faces were brighter than full moons with gleaming precious stones for eyes. There wasn't a down beat among them. As if on cue, the septet broke out into a barbershop rendition of the Battle Hymn of the Republic.

The audience was enthralled by the quality of their harmony and charisma. Applause was loud from old and young hands.

Resident Mel removed his bulldog mask and didn't Santa Claus appear, at least the face of the Christmas saint. His wheelchair was in the middle of the stage. He rotated it and said, "The Goldentones, ladies and gentlemen! Behind me from my right to the left are lovely Lisa, languorous Carol, laudable Ruth, lilting Winnie, lovely Jo Ann, legendary Alice and lively Linda." Each brought a straw hat from on high to heart and bowed to the audience. "Aren't they gorgeous tomatoes, folks!"

Goldentone Jo Ann came forward. "Thinking on tomatoes, Mel, why did one cross the garden?"

"Why?" He wore the look of a straight man.

"To get to the head of lettuce!" No matter the loud groan, Jo Ann tossed another. "Well then Mel, did you hear Nurse Belinda went to Medical Director Box to tell him Goldentone Carol needed to see him because she thought she was invisible?"

"No! Carol thought she was invisible?"

"Doc Box said to tell Carol he couldn't see her!"

Mel rotated his wheelchair again and pointed, "The Goldentones! And now the Sorcerers. To my left, Ann and Louis."

Ann removed a kitten mask, her face more along the lines of an old tiger's. Louis pulled off a louse's mask. His face, outlined by eyebrows and a moustache, carried a striking similarity to a bug's.

"To my right are Glendora and Otilla."

Glendora detached a sparrow mask to reveal a potato with dark eyes. Otilla disengaged from a falcon's mask, her own beak as sharp.

"Sorcerers!" Mel hollered."Question one. Is changing Social Security a big deal?"

"It sure is," Ann said, "FDR's New Deal got social security, Lyndon got Medicare, Nixon got Watergate, Ford got a wooden head; Carter got prayer; Reagan got Iran-Contra; the first Bush got new taxes; Clinton got a good return renting the Lincoln bedroom; and George the Second wants a choke hold on Social Security."

Otilla jumped in. "With big employers dropping pensions, if the second George gets his way, what's my son or daughter or grandchildren going to live on when they retire?"

Hearing about Social Security brought a buzzing reaction and the Goldentones up with a song: *"You're always a baby to mother, no matter how old you may grow'."*

"Question two," Mel shouted." What about Medicare Part D?"

"I'll tell you what about it," Louis said. "The government's not bargaining with the drug outfits, leaving bargaining up to insurers to negotiate."

"That's just like the United Nations did in that Food for Oil swap with Saddam," Glendora said. "He got kickbacks. The oil buyers got rich. Hungry folks stayed hungry."

"For sure," Louis said. "Drug companies and insurers won't be short on profits."

The Goldentones cut loose on that cue, "'Today Thy mercy Calls Us'. '"

"Thank you, thank you." Mel applauded along with the audience.

Then wasn't Jo Ann back! "Mel, what do you call fifty rabbits in a row? A hare line!"

"Wish Grandpa had one," Mel joked, pleased the audience appreciated his ab lib on the guest of honor. "Now to Question three!" Before the question poped out of Mel's mouth, his teeth did. He strained to reach the plate.

Otilla took the opportunity to make an observation. "Thanks to you Grandpa, none of us miss Elmer. When he and bookkeeper Lotta get sentenced, I hope they're tied to those Arabians and dragged across those acres out to the county line."

There is an awaking in the audience. Eyes cold as ice melt at the mention of the despised couple who used Medicaid money like it wasn't to be used.

"Remember whenever we would call Lotta?" Ann asked. "She had one of those phones that gave instructions. 'For the balance in your personal needs account, push one; for the price of a cup of vending machine coffee, push two;' and Elmer's favorite, 'for failure to pay your liability, pack.'"

The audiences' reaction amazed the Sorcerers. Eyes were stars, mouths' caves of delight.

Glendora kept it up. "Doc Box examined me the other week and gave me two aspirin. Elmer said he'd bill Medicaid in the morning."

"How do you define a nursing home 'administrator'?" Louis had his own answer. "One skilled in getting around State Health survey inspections."

"Once I went into Elmer's office," Ann said, "to talk about my birthday party. He wouldn't let me celebrate it."

"He would have," Otilla said. "You just wouldn't wait for the maintenance man to pull in the hose before the candles were lit."

"Elmer wasn't all bad," Louis said. "When he came in to my room answering Glen's call, Elmer took me go to the toilet, no matter Glen was on it."

"I know all about going to the bathroom," Mel said after returning his lower plate. "Our bodily functions change for the worse as we get older, so I don't dare light up a cigarette after liver and onions."

"Don't talk about the food Elmer's cooks dished up," Otilla said. "Just hearing about them curdles my ear wax."

"Ever notice how Elmer's therapists billed for their time?" Louis said. "They billed for time putting on the white coat, walking the hall to my room, checking to see if I'm warm, writing down those observations and time checking if the fifteen minutes were up.

"Before State Health took over running the nursing home," Mel said, "I overheard Elmer telling Lotta 'your job is to keep the place full and residents paying their liability. So keep an eye on the charge nurses and Aides. They want to get the residents up and out.'"

Aides and nurses applauded in appreciation.

"Well, some of us got better," Ann said. "Last month old Joe and Big Sophie felt so good after their medicines, they got to throwing punches in Activities, but Elmer wouldn't stop it. He had Big Sophie at ten to one."

"What about my care plan," Otilla said. "Elmer had them work up my Minimum Data Set and gave me a bum RAP."

That inside joke got nurses' glee and the Goldentones into '*Ain't that Good News.*'

Before Jo Ann was up again, Mel shouted, "Question Four: Is Medicaid in danger?"

"Thinking on Medicaid money," Glendora said, "they made sure I spent all my cash before picking up the nursing home tab. Elmer got back at them for me. He took it for all he could."

"You got to admit," Mel said, "that Elmer brought the nursing home up to date with technology. Push the call button to go to the bathroom, and you get all five movements of Beethoven's Ninth Symphony."

"Beethoven's Ninth has only four movements, Mel," Glendora said.

"Waiting on someone to answer my call button, there was five."

The Goldentones broke out with *'Cleanse Me, O Lord, I humbly plead.'*

Jo Ann wasn't to be denied, coming up on Mel's shoulder before the last line of the song faded. "Remember when we had a portable x-ray machine and Elmer sneaked in and x-rayed himself? It showed only lungs. 'Where's my heart?' Elmer asked."

"Wasn't in his work, for sure," Ann said. "That was confirmed when Doc Box gave Elmer a mental test. It took only a minute."

"Doc sure knew about Elmer, but not much on diagnoses," Otilla said.

"But he came around a lot," Glendora argued.

"He had to," Otilla said, "he needed the practice."

"Doc said he'd given me my shot," Louis said. "Is that why my jigger was empty?'"

"Who ever is elected president of the resident

council," Mel said, "should hold a 'take your favorite 'Doctor to Dinner' day.'"

"Is Doc Box your favorite doctor?" Otilla asked.

"Dr. Ruth is!"

"What's the difference between a nursing home administrator, and an Aide?" Glendora probed. "About seventy five thousand dollars a year."

Aides hooted as if one.

"My daughter Mary was in to see Elmer to discuss my monthly bill," Ann said. "When Elmer said, 'let's be honest.' Mary said, 'you go first'. That ended the discussion."

"What do you call a circular nurse station?" Mel said. "It's a dope ring."

Charge nurses moaned.

"What's a nursing home attorney?" Otilla inquired. "One who bites the hands that feeds us, Medicaid."

"Isn't it strange medical doctors don't like to work with nursing home residents, but yet so many hold ownership positions in nursing homes?" Mel said. "Why?"

"Because their speciality is surgery of Medicaid's wallet," Otilla said.

"Did you read any of Elmer's old adverts telling about how good Union Township nursing home was for old folks to come live here?" Ann asked. "They won the top prize for fiction!"

Applause is as loud as feeble old hands can make it, like wounded bird wings flapping.

"Why, when Elmer ran the home, was the new

bathing facility so busy?" Louis asked.

"Because he had to drive through to wash his Cadillac!" Otilla said.

"What happens to unused medicines when a resident passes?" Mel inquired.

"Elmer destroyed them at his office parties," Louis said.

"I remember when a lot of residents got inflatable posture vests," Louis said, "so they could sit straight in their wheelchairs. How much did it cost you, Glendora?"

"Nothing," she said. "It was a Christmas gift. Elmer and the salesman said 'Merry Christmas from Medicare!'"

"What was the difference between Elmer's janitors and Elmer's cooks?" Mel said. "Nothing. Both threw out their work product. Belinda's new ones are good, though!"

"How many of Elmer's Aides were needed to help a resident from bed to her wheel chair?" Otilla said.

"One!" Ann said. "There weren't any more around. Not so since Belinda got to hiring. In the chapel you can now hear the angels singing when an Aide comes in."

"Still, crime pays," Mel said. "Elmer's doings got Grandpa talking to the ombudsman, and that got us Belinda and new hires on the floor, in the kitchen and on clean up."

The walls echoed with applause for Grandpa. He was too embarrassed to stand up.

The Goldentones closed the show with, *'Oh, Sing With Exultation'*."

PROPOSAL

A hard day's work on the back acres of Noah's and Hezikiah's farms was rewarded when Homer, the Hired Man, passed the word of invite to come over to his Mama's for fresh baked pumpkin pie. Grandpa too, for he'd helped with mucking.

A third piece of that there mouth-watering pie must have put a spell on Noah, the widower, who looked up from his plate with mouth full and said, "Delicta, I love you - - -." The rest was muffled when he sputtered pumpkin on to his bib overalls.

Delicta, the old tomato with no neck, as round of face and body as the super sized watermelons and pumpkins she nurtured in her garden, leapt from her chair with a handy dish cloth to wipe goo, baby like, from Noah's lips and overalls, then fell on his neck as if to guillotine him. She smothered the befuddled grain farmer in her squash, splashed him with kisses and as much as squeezed tooth paste out of him.

"I love you too, Noah," she said to misty eyes and gaping lips. "We can have our wedding over to Holy Smoke Church, this Saturday morning."

Hezikiah, Grandpa and Homer were rendered dumb. Was Noah out of his mind saying those words, or was it the heat of a day's harvest of soybeans?

Breath slow to come back, Noah's hiss was hard to hear, "Delicta, I said I love you for your pumpkin pie."

Hezikiah and Grandpa heard him. Noah's love was for the pumpkin, the one that was a baked pie, not for tying a knot to Delicta tighter than the hangman's.

She revised a choke hold, the grain farmer gasping again until she released her newly found beau and stood over him, shaking her hinder acres.

"No need to wait longer to soothe them feeling folks have what are hot on each other."

She hadn't heard Noah's hissing explanation, Grandpa decided. If she believed Noah had the hots for her, she'd ignored the crossing of his eyes, lips parting like Moses' Red Sea, head bobbing and straps of his overalls slipping off his shoulders. They weren't heartening indications.

Delicta, however, read all as witness to ready passion, him being a widower so long.

She was on horseback charging to the bridal path.

Hezikiah mind was so caught up with the opportunity to fun his neighbor, even if on oath, the dairy farmer wouldn't testify before Judge Stodgy up to the County Court House that he'd overheard Noah's hissing it was the pie he coveted, not Delicta.

If Homer heard it, his silence confirmed he feared a skewing if a word against the nuptials was said by Mama's own kin.

Grandpa remained mute, not knowing how to plead Noah's plight to the joyous woman in her own kitchen with immediate access to knives. Speed flaunted in his dotage walking the back roads wasn't up to ducking any sharp edge of Delicta's butcher knife. Better safe than sliced baloney.

"I'll make arrangements with Clem over to Holy Smoke church," Delicta said releasing Noah from her fierce grip.

Homer took it on himself to leave his piece of pie unprotected to get up and lean on Delicta's ear to whisper, "Mama. I thought you was sweet on Reverend Clem, seeing as he was going to get you on as his relief van driver over to Union Township nursing home."

"He ain't said no words like that there Noah did, has he?" She whispered in return.

"I've got a good idea," Hezikiah said hopping up like a kangaroo. "A bachelor party for Noah over to my barn Friday after second milking."

"And a bridal shower Friday morning!" Homer exclaimed.

"Women do bridal showers," Hezikiah said disgustedly, "not my hired man. Have some pride."

"Womens?" Homer said, face as red as Hezikiah's suspenders.

"Don't rightly need that there bridal shower," Delicta said, "got me all kinds of stuff."

"How about the engagement ring, Ma?" Homer said looking at Noah.

"Forget it. Bought back the one your Pa pawned before he turned over the pickup. He never could drive right on roads. Safe as hell in the demolition derbies."

"Who's your best man, Noah," Hezikiah said,

pushing the button of levity

Noah was too stupefied to reply, react or retreat. Whether it was from near suffocation when pushed between Mama's squash, or shock over Delicta's love onslaught, or the quicky marriage, or all combined, he hadn't his right mind, whatever that was.

"Come on, Noah," Grandpa said to rescue the befuddled groom. He put his hands under the stunned man's armpits to lift him to his feet, walking him as if he were an old codger.

"Homer," Delicta ordered, "you keep a close eye out for my next mate, you hear!"

"Yea, Mama."

The three, Grandpa, Hezikiah and Homer helped Noah outside where fresh air revived him in contrast to Delicta's sharp breath that knocked him for a loop.

"What happened?" Noah asked.

"You getting hitched to Delicta on Saturday," Hezikiah said, exaulting.

"Hitched?"

"That's right," Hezikiah said, "day after tomorrow, Saturday."

"Saturday! She proposed?"

"You did," Homer cut in. "You told Mama you loved her, and she went along."

"I proposed?" Beads of sweat formed on Noah's forehead, dripping on his jutting chin.

Hezikiah was having a difficult time not reveling out loud. "Your manner of speaking to Delicta was took as a proposal," he said. "Bachelor party tomorrow over to my barn after second milking. Homer's going to bring Yukon Jack to get you ready for nuptial night."

"Nuptial night! Co-op, help me!" Noah gasped. "I ain't going thought with it."

"You be!" Homer said, puffed up like a shotgun rider on a stagecoach.

A double take taken at Delicta's beet-red face son, Noah backed away.

Grandpa cut between them. "Hold on a minute, Homer. There's no marriage license. Can't have a wedding without a marriage license."

"What you saying, Grandpa," Homer said. "All kinds of folks in Union Township be living together without one of them marriage licenses."

"Don't worry your mind about a wedding license, Grandpa," Hezikiah said mirthfully "Pastor Clem is best friend to County Commissioner Rummy. He'll get it for Clem, seeing as how he swings his congregation Rummy's way come election."

"That's right," Homer said, relived. "Pastor Clem gets the license, marry them right. You'll be my Pa, Noah."

"Oh my," he moaned, a double take given Homer.

"See you tomorrow, Noah," Homer said with a hint of command. "I be coming to pick you up after second milking, sure enough!"

Grandpa detected Hezikiah was over enjoying himself. Was he caught up with funning Noah at a bachelor party like he had the former city slicker at church suppers?

Surely so!

"Let's go, Noah," Grandpa said, a plan crossing his mind, one he'd play out at the bachelor party. "Seeing as I walked over to Delicta's, let me have your pickup keys, Noah. I'll drive you to your place. Walk back to mine."

Next day, Grandpa made the walk to Hezikiah's barn that dated to homestead times. Where there had been a milking room, cheese-making room and a scullery, there were the benches on which local folks sat when Grandpa went to Court before Justice of the Peace Homer. The court was a hoax planned by Hezikiah and Deputy Duty to fun Grandpa over a ticket for failure to hang a red reflective triangle on his hinder quarters when walking public roads.

The scenery the other side of the barn remained the south side of dairy cows looking north.

Underneath the hay loft, where the front seat of a Model A was perched on several hay bales, Homer and Noah sat as if tied, each fisting a glass of Yukon Jack. Hezikiah was standing, his drink on a hay bale, clapping hands to the tune of Mississippi Mud playing on his Victrola as Minerva, waitress from Lila's Café, pole danced, albeit, wearing jeans and a wet t-shirt. No matter her outfit, Minerva was a well formed woman making her fortune moonlighting, even though the night's dark was a touch away.

"Come on, Noah," Hezikiah yelled over the music, "take a look at Minerva, and dream when you see your bride tomorrow night."

Noah shook his head mournfully.

Homer tensed, being as Mama was the bride, not Minerva.

"Come get a gander of this here dancing chick, Grandpa," Hezikiah hollered wiggling his ample rear in time with Minerva's movements, fore and after.

"Come dance with me. Come on!" Minerva shrieked.

It could be said Hezikiah had in mind Minerva was shaking herself to warm up Noah for the upcoming nuptials, but it was him that was warmer. "Sure enough," he said.

No sooner than the well developed waitress was working Hezikiah like he was a milk shake, than the barn door flew opened. Reverend Clem, the Holy Smoke church Pastor and part time van driver over to the nursing home, entered. Following, were a moving convoy of well aged ladies using walkers or rolling wheel chairs.

After them came Zelma, Hezikiah's wife, and the bride to be, Delicta. Zelma's nose veins turned as red as those running the tracks on her ears when she saw the dancing. She hollered, "let loose, Hezikiah!"

"This be a bachelor party," he yelled, holding on. "Git out of here!"

"I said, let go." When Zelma picked up a pitchfork, there was a parting of the ways.

"Aren't these ladies the Goldentones from the nursing home?" Grandpa said as if surprised.

"They are," Reverend Clem said, "come to sing."

"For Noah and Delicta?" Grandpa.said.

"For me," Reverend Clem answered.

On cue, the Goldentones clustered up like light bulbs on a Christmas tree; five with walkers around two in wheelchairs. They ran the decades from seven to half eight, with eyes brighter than Hezikiah's at Minerva. Then they broke into:

"The voice that breathed over Eden, that earliest wedding day,

"The primal marriage blessing, it had not passed away."

Harmony soothing all but Hezikiah, Reverend Clem fell to a knee before Delicta. He said, "Be marrying me, Delicta, not yon farmer. Marrying another of that kind will be as bad as the first. Come be a Pastor's wife and assistant van driver."

"I say you're doing right nice by me, Pastor," Delicta said, "but, Noah done asked first"

Due to the astonishing turn around, Noah was fully sober and in full possession of his senses, Yukon Jack, or no. "Like Reverend Clem done say, Delicta. Getting hitched to another farmer is one too many share cropers. I free you."

"Hallelujah," Reverend Clem exclaimed.

"Right nice of you, Noah," Delicta said, blushing.

"I be that kind of man," he said, and fainted.

GRANDPA'S GOLF GAME

Grandpa, back in the1940s, after World War II was won, was a slick fourteen year old lad, if you can conjure the old geezer being young, who, when summer came on, assuming no summer school for a change, caddied at Plum Hollow Golf Course. It weren't but a long bike ride from his home at Murray Hill Street on Detroit's Northwest side. Caddies had the privilege on Mondays to play golf, but the old, er, young coot didn't. Why? It came down to playing or caddying for Detroit Tiger baseball players on Major League Baseball's day off. A hard choice?

Duh! Slicing that little white tablet to the wrong fairway weren't a thought in Grandpa's dwarfish mind when Hal Newhouser, Dizzy Trout, pitchers, Paul Richards and Birdie Tebbets, catchers, asked if he were interested in caddying for one of them. Weak of mind, a natural failing, but strong of back with good Irish genes, Grandpa offered to caddy for the entire heroic foursome. Fortunately, there was pity took by them Big Leaguers on the awe struck booby, restraining the red head, he had a lot of hair then, to Hal Newhouser's golf bag which weighed slightly less than the club house. Weren't of no matter to the teen-ager, later Grandpa. He would have carried Newhouser and his baseball equipment too, if'en the left handed pitcher wanted to ride his golf bag like a saddle on a goat.

At all shots in the rough, bunkers or sand traps on them 18 holes, accompanied with grunts and wheezes, one or all of them big leaguers loudly and with thought before and after the fact violently expressed themselves! Grandpa heard up close language he hadn't heard in a crowd at Briggs Stadium whenever Newhouser, Trout, Tebbets or Richards warmly addressed an Umpire after a wrong call at the plate. A Detroit Tiger weren't never wrong, just umps, bedeviled as they were with lousy eyesight.

Grandpa could have turned his attention to the lofty, seeing as he were one of them scholars what had showed up for eight grade classes every single day at St. Scholastica Grade School, much to the regret of Sister Mary Monster. (There were questions in the boys' lavatory about Sister's gender seeing as she had a right cross to the head like to knock out more than baby teeth).

As Birdie Tebbets and Paul Richards had just returned from military service, Grandpa found more than one hollow in his mentality to store them tangy phrases until his own military time happened and he rose up the ranks, wistful thought, and were a sergeant trained to use them properly. Them words that belonged to Major leaguers who was former soldiers, served Sergeant Grandpa well when the time for combat in Korea were ripe. But reader, you ain't got a license to use them words until exalted to the rank of Sergeant in the United States Army. Sergeants be true professionals when caressing words.

This here Plum Hollow tale had a good twist, though, not for Grandpa taking up them words, but being asked to caddie every time Newhouser had a Monday off. Sure enough, Grandpa took him up on it! Hal, a lefty, even went so far as to show Grandpa, a right hander, how to use a driver off the tee; hit an approach shot; pop a chip, put from the sinister side. Them who study people's physical peculiarities would say Grandpa, already distinct in that category, got a heavy dose of cross pollination on summer's Monday golf instructions, albeit looking into a mirror, opposite so to speak.

After Hal's parables that there magic summer, Grandpa, (he had a touch of vigor back then), put in a touch of caddie shack golfing after delivery of the Detroit Free Press newspaper in the mornings and before afternoon baseball practice. Somehow, he lumbered through grade school, got by in high school, and when admission standards were lower than the bed of a dry creek, bambozzled through two years of college, holding back them learned words until the military where they came in handy when he finally made sergeant.

His own Ma and Pa were stunned Grandpa went back to higher education and that he finished it without expulsion. They were astonished but showed up at the awarding of a dead sheep's skin. Didn't mean nothing to them, seeing as the writing on the skin was in the language of dead Romans. None-the-less, Grandpa's Ma and Pop figured on it a while, a vision telling them their son had a future, a vision wistful beyond reality. Still, they conferred on him tools necessary to lift him up, eventually, to America's lower middle class. They gave their daft son a set of golf clubs, that he might be numbered among swells. Grandpa's folks anticipated their lad, educated way beyond his intelligence, would ultimately walk, not public golf courses, but private country clubs' close cut grass with the giants of commerce.

Lacking revenue to underwrite any golf club's membership, it took more cash than the price of Grandpa's first bought house over on the depreciated Northwest side of Detroit, he nonetheless took up his golf clubs with low rung social climbers and walked the roughs, sand traps and bunkers of public links. Grandpa rarely walked a fairway! This here were his excuse: Hal Newhouser's left handed legacy dominated a right handed swing. No need to cotton to that alibi! Old goat Grandpa's swing were worse than a rusty garden gate's falling off hinges.

Came his former classmates' invitation to a round of golf. Grandpa took a turn off the tees alright, but his elegant presence was apart from the rest of the foursome the yardage each hole from tee to green, exasperation of the others glowing like traffic lights in the dark. This round were more than wearisome for Grandpa, like carrying a full field pack and weapon up one of them forty-five degree hills in Korea. Wishing to be reacquainted with his old buddies, instead he made acquaintance with trees, rough, creeks and sand traps bordering or crossing fairways, obstructing approaches to greens. Divots flew and not a bird or wild thing above or below ground chanced life or limb. When Grandpa finally got the battered but smiling golf ball on a green, weren't his put always away! His everlasting putting caused cadavers to cool, tempers steam, waiting a turn to put before the sun set and the moon rose.

(Heard tell them PGA golfers be embarrassed they three put a green. Grandpa whooped and hollered over a low six like he scored a touchdown.)

That were his last 18 holes! Offering up golfing as atonement for pungent phrases taught by Major Leaguers and absorbed by an awestruck caddie, practiced when licensed as a sergeant and raucously recalled each hole of the final round, Grandpa deposited his golf swing's phenomenal banana slice, (often offset by a thunderous hook), and his clubs into a slumber. It rivaled Rumpelstiltskin's.

After years in the work queue, but hoping to punch retirement's time clock before his own, Grandpa took big buttocks, off to Union Township to retire on a red wood chair on the front porch of an old farm house on a back acre country road. Couldn't get much farther from big city folks, could he? What a sight! Farmer Noah's corn to the south and soy beans north, if'en Grandpa ever turned his head around to look south. T'weren't no need to turn yearly. It were the opposite planting next season. Not so farmer Hezekiah's Holsteins to the west. Winds waffled daily delights of fertilized countryfied air, to say nothing of the waffling fragrances that floated freely each twist of the wind from Hired Man and Hired dog!

Grandpa sat a decade of rapturous repose on that there red wood chair on the front porch before the big crash done come. It weren't a crash of them pickups that raced the back roads and did dirt to 'possums slow crossing east to west on the road north to south, nor a tractor's plow furrowing a graveled lane, nor the market them rich fellows on Wall street schemed about, Grandpa hadn't no money there nohow, nor were it a upturn in flatulence from Hezekiah's milk cows.

It were farmer Noah who crashed the peace of the porch when he came calling and scattered delirium, like whopping Grandpa's head just below where the two hairs parted like the Red Sea. Noah had no time to take up relaxation the long years of planting crops, except to cat-fish in his stocked pond. He told he'd gone and sold a heapful of acres to an entrepreneur not a specialist in bovine manure. Noah recollected the big buck negotiations with them slickers, (he took them), but he weren't real clear on what they had up their sleeves. He heard tell they was to build eighteen plantation size yards and drill a hole in each, a lot of wells, sure enough, and buy as many flags. Patriotic, wasn't them rich folks? And the fields would be cut so close a farmer might reckon a great flock of sheep worked them, never mind the droppings. When all was said and done, paying folks, dressed colorful like to fight bulls, would come to walk them plantation yards of Mystic Hills, so they labeled them back acres, and drink of the deep pumped water. Stranger than wishing on eighteen wells! Them pretty folks would carry a bag of big sticks like they was to fend off critters. Weren't! (This to tell of next were hard for Noah to imagine.) Each of them folks were going to hit their own balls! Head shaking in wonder, Noah understood why they then had to run to powered carts, (who could walk), and drive wild like leaves in a whirl wind. Noah concluded his narration telling he sure looked forward to watching them do themselves mischief!

Sweet cider bringing on a quiet, Grandpa schooled Noah on golf's tees, fairways, rough, traps and putting greens; that the balls smacked weren't of the manly variety. The carts, getting in and out, were fat man's exercise from green to green. Plantation yards, where balls were to fall into a cup and finally come to rest in the hole, were greens, flag marked.

Noah thought hitting a golf ball with sticks just to plunge it into a flag hole wouldn't be no test like to dropping a moth ball on a string down a black snake hole. Still, not having to stretch legs from hole to hole had a good side. He opined to get his big body in gear and practice with them sticks and balls over on his back forty, and buy him one of them golf carts to get ready for roaring over cut grass and chipmunk holes. He'd be proud, come the opening in a couple of years, to cart four big cheeks, his'n, seven with Grandpa, from hole to hole, sticks a slashing, balls a popping!

Grandpa's eyes uncrossed, ears flapped at Noah's canny comments. A thought tickled the red chair sitter's cement head. Were he up to pulling splinters out his backside and rising once again to swing his ancient woods and irons? At Noah's parting, Grandpa unraveled tired shoulders, stringy arms and stiffen fingers, what with arthritis having clawed them up, and time after time sneaked off to town's practice range. He would have game, something he ain't never had before.

Meanwhile, didn't Grandpa watch, even turn his head, as tractors and shovels moved mounds of dirt to make mountains and them fellows build greens like pool tables and planted particles of finely cut grass, slick slivers of fairways growing close by raspy herbage, near to weed choked rough and woods. Them fellows damned creeks, fertilized swamps and hauled in sand to monster traps, sand deep enough to rival a quarter thousand of kindergarten sand boxes. Afterwards they cut paths, flattened a mound for a practice tee, graveled a parking lot and herded carts into a coral. Next, they rolled in a trailer and opened doors. Inside, pretty ladies what could write, school house learned, writ names in a book of playing times after a touch of folks' pocketbooks.

Grandpa put his practice to the test early of a morning, there being none of them cart herders on the tee to comment on his swing. He swung, swung, and swung again, the three misses warm ups and of no account, just the fourth which zinged the golf ball forward a good two hundred yards before slicing another hundred and landing near to the sixth fairway. Trouble were, Grandpa were on the first hole! He pulled his cart, not his natural trailer, but the one on wheels carrying his hitting sticks over to the white speck he'd dumped there and lashed at it like to trash it good. It flew high up, near to hit a circling hawk, and come down where the sand trap got no bottom.

Now there ain't no meanness intended in this here story, so there ain't no need to tell how the old geezer dug himself a foxhole in that there sand fit for a rifleman, or the golf ball flew over the green more times than the cow jumped the moon, or putts rolled sideways and crossways, nary a one straight to the hole. Though it were his first time out in nigh on forty years, it seemed bad habits of long ago golf lived longer than expected!

Grandpa persevered that there first season. Got to the point his drive's slice weren't no worse than a banana's curve, his three woods off roughs, (rarely on fairways), was hooks like the back of them bananas, long irons fluttered like string beans, middle irons ricocheted off grass, pitches were tossed shorter than camels' humps, chips flew stubbier than cows' droppings, and putts, they was blind to the flag.

There weren't an ounce of quit in Grandpa, never smart despite that there college education, so he would have another go the next season. He snuck out, beforehand, to that course of golfs and lashed away every day of Union Township's one hour of winter daylight, no matter the three foot of snow or zero cold.

He did all that just to get game!

Well, there is a happy ending to this tale of golfs.

Grandpa never got game, par 71, or even 81 or 91.

What he got was five to seven miles of walking over eighteen holes, the way the old goat walked from tee to green: sideways, backwards, across, over, down, up, in, out, and finally forward.

Grandpa hadn't game, but he got legs!

MYSTICAL THIRTEENTH

Grandpa's golf ball faded, finding soft earth near a thick forest. It wasn't a magic wand, it was his driver the old duffer waved on the tee of the par four 13th at Mystic Hills golf course. Waving as if to ward off a swarm of mosquitoes, he frightened a family of cranes. They hurriedly moved away. Remorse touched him, something new for one already touched, for frightening the feeding long legged birds.

Was his golf game down to scaring birds, not making par, never a birdie on the 13th?

He wondered why he was walking and lugging a golf bag with fourteen clubs every morning, dragging a sorry body the miles of eighteen holes into trees and weeds where snakes took the shade. Walking miles on Union Township's paved roads was easier, there being nothing but flatten snakes, racked racoons and squashed squirrels.

What was there about the 13th hole?

His answer came in a vision.

He saw a fairway with a ridge line bisecting it, on the north side of which was a far away green. The side to the left of the fairway was covered with fog as thick as a raging fire's smoke. The opposite side's swamp had eight foot tall reeds. A bitter wind was blowing and driving the fog and reeds in all directions. He saw golf balls, like hailstones in the fury of a tempest, hooking, fading, flying back and forth from one side of the fairway's rough to the other.

By the green, the light was dim as if in a nocturnal, solitary gloom. Frequent masses of pulverized sand spouted around it, rising from great pits, falling back endlessly.

Golfers were down in the pits, swinging sand irons, golf balls like sparks rising up with smoke flying high into the air, dropping back into the pits.

He heard hideous sounds and desperate lamentations accompanied by hard laughter and mocking voices. Those who were weeping were down in the pits, those on the green were laughing.

On the sloping green, when laughing golfers putted, their golf balls became glowing eyes, watering, going by the cup and rolling into the pits.

He heard hideous sounds and desperate lamentations accompanied by hard laughter and mocking voices. Those who had putted were now weeping from the pits. Those who had been in the pits were now laughing up on the green.

Frequent masses of pulverized sand spouted again and again, rising from the great pits, falling back endlessly, golf balls like sparks rising up with smoke flying high into the air, dropping back. On the sloping green, golf balls, when golfers putted, became glowing eyes, watering, going by the cup and rolling into the pits.

It was an unending cycle!

There was an odor of verbal sulphur rising from the pits and the green.

Duffers' Hell?

Vision over, Grandpa took a double bogey and got out of there.

EAGLE, BIRDIE, GOOSE

Goose?

Playing a round on Mystic Hills golf course, when low handicap golfers score birdies or pars, it's expected. When one scores an eagle, it's celebrated around the club house as a big deal.

A big deal? When last was there club house revelry over a goose?

That's right, a goose! Before drinks are bought for the house over an old duffer Grandpa's accomplishment, some perspective is called for.

All old duffers think their making a birdie is a bigger deal than a low handicap golfer's eagle. Why? Old duffers like Grandpa don't reach many greens in regulation. Their best hope to birdie is on a par three.

Take the 3rd when topped a line drive that shot from the tee, bounced off the fairway to the green, finding its way to a foot from the hole's front placement flag. Even then, lining up the tap-in putt, Grandpa fought off choking up, a nerve wracking ordeal.

But it was a birdie!

A birdie on Grandpa's score card looked heroic, a number less than the printed number, a spectacular number symbolic of great shots, a turn around of one no longer to be numbered at the bottom of woods and rough wanderers.

All old duffers like Grandpa don't sneeze on the making of pars, either. Recording the same number the score card indicated is expected, is ego boosting.

A good hole for Grandpa to par is the 7th. If his drive off the tee to the south clears the east to west deep bisecting ditch and lands on the fairway right of the 100 foot long sand trap and left of the south to north creek that swallows slices, it's possible he can get a second shot on the green in regulation. That shot needs to avoid the green's eastern high side and the sand trap on the west. Hopefully the pin placement is somewhere near the front to two putt for par. As luck has it, most times there's sixty-five feet to lag over mounds to get a view of the 7th hole pin placement.

Now about that goose.

Its comes to most cart riding golfers' attention there isn't a goose on the front nine, but on the back nine down by the wetlands geese number several couples who flaunt their offspring by parading on the 10th fairway, the 11th tee and the 15th green as if at Culver's Lake Fest. Geese pollution could be a problem, but isn't, because the maintenance crew, Earl, Truman, Willie and Roy run machines that pulverize droppings to fertilizer.

On the front nine, before Grandpa took on the back nine marching queues, he hit his driver with abandon off the 9th tee, a line drive fit to be a triple in any Major League ball park. It rode the west side of the fairway heading toward the far end of the long, deep sand bunker.

Geese?

Grandpa's shot hit the last goose in a line of ambling geese heading west.

Geese on the 9th? No longer! There was evacuation!

Both up in the air and some left on the fairway.
   The golf ball? It ricocheted into play.
   That's a goose!

NIGHT GUARD

As if fleeing Deputy Duty, Noah's and Hezikiah's pickups turned right smartly off the back road, one after the other, into the driveway, sliding to stops, shedding small stones every which way but back to Grandpa's driveway.

He hurried from the porch to the commotion. "What's going on," he hollered off the back steps. "You fleeing the Law?"

Noah, opening the driver side door, jumped from his truck and yelled, not to Grandpa but to Hezikiah and Homer, the Hired Man, "told you my truck's engine can beat anything old Homer rebuilds."

"Just lucky," Homer answered.

"Lucky?" said Hezikiah to Homer. "You need to rev up this here hunk of junk, if'en I'm going to run that there plow puller off the road, you hear?"

Homer didn't come back to Hezikiah, but turned to Grandpa and said, "told Hezikiah and Noah about that there cootie hunt when you was in Korea."

Noah said, "I didn't know you was a soldier in the Korean War, Grandpa, until Homer went on about them cooties. Never was drafted to the military, Hezikiah neither. Deferred, being we was farmers. Homer, too."

Hezikiah said, "My hired man couldn't pass the written test, no how."

A look given by Homer to Hezikiah's throat was as if he was holding it tightly between two cold hands. "Could too."

"Anyhow Grandpa," Noah said, "we come on over, so fill us in on Korea."

"Come on in, men. Have a seat out to the porch while I fetch a jug of Yukon Jack."

Bib overalls on parade, they ambulated through the kitchen, dining room, TV room and out the door to the front porch as if at home, and took to seating to relax on Grandma's new wicker chairs, softened with pillow seats.

Jug in hand, four glasses clinging to the other hand's fingers, Grandpa set a glass down, poured a few fingers, moved on to two, three and wasn't about to forget himself. Chores done, being as it was every man for himself after first pour, he took his leisure on the red wood chair.

"The war over there lasted three years, from June 1950 to July 1953," Grandpa said. "What I'm going to go on about happened in April 1952. My outfit was on the front line in an area called the Punch Bowl, north of the 38th parallel where Korea was even more mountainous with long ridge lines and slopes that ran down from the peak of hills like fingers from a hand. I was where rumors floated like leaves in a stream. Top on the rumor list was Chinese Commie infiltrators, we called them night crawlers, who aimed to kidnap any GI found off his guard."

"Co-op help them," Noah said, his face already anticipating Grandpa's capture and heroic escape.

"My outfit was Dog Company, 1st Battalion of the 35th Regimental Combat team, 25th Infantry Division. My section of heavy machine guns was part of the Main Line of Resistance. I was a squad leader, finally, after six months as a gunner, and had placed my squad's machine guns down a finger to get maximum fire power where I expected the Commies would hit."

"A machine gunner?" Said Hezikiah. "I had an Uncle out of Kewanna who was a machine gunner during World War I." His face reflected worry. Would Grandpa get hit by enemy shelling like his uncle?

"In the Autumn of 1951, my regiment launched attacks against the enemy, inflicting casualties while taking only a few. Then, in the late fall we were ordered to dig in when the truce talks perked up. Was that it? The end of the Korean war? I figured GIs and Commies needed only to watch each other from opposing lines from then on.

"But, as every enlisted man in the Army expected, an officer was assigned the duty of finding things that need not be done and thus could be done over and over. For sure, this Officer had the battalion, and others, running combat patrols to prove we hadn't lost our will to fight. Battalion troops attacked the high point, ran the Commies off, held the hill, beat off counterattacks, then pulled off. Sure enough, within a few days the Commies re-occupied."

Homer visualized throwing grenades like he threw baseballs off the mound.

"Both sides, Commies and GIs, were equally disgusted with the number of rats around our bunkers. Those rodents thrived on the war, increased and multiplied during trench warfare. No one was paid to shoot them, but from time to time I wasn't the only one who squeezed off a round. It was a losing battle. The rats had more replacements than the enemy.

"My attention to finalizing the existence of a few more rodents was interrupted when Sergeant Warren, carbine drawn, came down the trench line chewing out the GI in front of him. The soldier wasn't mute, letting out vile phrases directed at the United States Army and the big sergeant who was chiding him.

"I met them at Dog Two gun hole and was told I had a new replacement. At the sergeant's departure, George, the new guy, vulgarity his native lingo, told all present at Dog Two, back stateside he'd been a truck mechanic. He claimed the motor pool was his Military Occupational Speciality, not heavy weapons. He said he'd been dealt a dirty deal. He was visibly shaking.

"I paid little mind to the grouching for what infantryman hadn't felt he'd been given the shaft in the form of fighting at the end of a bayonet on an M1 Rifle. I introduced himself and the guys in the squad, telling George my squad manned three machine gun bunkers. I told George that Clouse, Grezgorek and I were to the left in Dog One. Brooks, Alexander and Truscott to the right in Dog Three. George would be in Dog Two with Rosenbloom and Im Ta Song, a Republic of Korea soldier, Joe ROK we called him, who was assigned to Dog Company.

"Rosenbloom didn't leave well enough alone. He told nervous George that Commie night crawlers had infiltrated Easy Company last night and kidnaped a GI.

"There was a long silence. George looked at Grandpa, Rosenbloom and then at Joe ROK. Seeing the Korean soldier, George expressed a few befouled opinions about people of that descent, and while doing it, became highly agitated, shaking nervously. His Adam's apple bounced like a fishing bob. George's eyes were white, watery and wide. Joe ROK was stoic.

"It made little difference to Rosenbloom that George was distraught when he was put on first night guard. It was to the advantage of buddies in the sleeping bunker that the night guard in the fighting bunker was highly alert.

"That night, the wind whooshed and whistled over the line and down drafts played about the bunker, popping ponchos covering entrances. The rear echelon search lights came across the line to light up the clouds over no man's land. The light reflected downwardly, illuminating both sides of the front line and increasing shadows and anxiety. As the clouds moved, the light seemingly walked across the valley, changing known forms into unknown. C-ration cans, hung on the barbed wire to rattle when disturbed, rattled. A particularly good wind could stir up a band of cans. Even an experienced GI's imagination could be so spooked he would whistle an alert over the communication telephone. It was always followed by a parachute flare and a coarse request to settle down and let the command bunker alone.

"On fourth shift, two hours on, four off, I came on

guard in Dog One, Brooks in Dog Three, and Joe ROK, with a torrent of Korean words flooding the sleeping bunker, forcing George out and back to the fighting hole. Rosenbloom cursed George mightily, again, venting feelings about being awaken several times on George's first shift.

"The rats were out in force. They slipped around the side of my bunker and ran along the top of the communication trench that ran west up toward Dog Two. I didn't know it at the time, but George hadn't been informed of the rats. Rosenbloom's indoctrination had covered the gun holes, communication system and other soldierly duties befalling a front line troop, but he forgot to mention the rats.

"Rats seemed to have sensed an intense element of fear from Dog Two and called a convention at the site. Coming through the roof at the gun bunker, rats knocked dirt onto George's helmet. He jumped and his helmet fell. The startled rats jumped in response. George gasped loudly as he sucked in air, sounding as if choked.

"When Brooks up in Dog Three heard the gasp, he came out of his gun hole to look down the trench towards Dog Two. He hollered. No response.

"The rats fled the roof, jumping to the sides of the gun bunker to scurry out of the shooting port past George. Their sudden movement, and man's instinctive dislike for rats, and the soldier's for surprise, caused George to tear the air with a loud guttural sob.

"Brooks figured Commie night crawlers had the

new guy, so he hurled an illuminating grenade down the communication trench. It burst right by Dog Two bunker. George saw the flash and let out a piercing cry.

"I remember I was looking out my gun port down the finger toward the Commies' lines when I caught sight of the flash. I grabbed my M1 carbine.

"When Brooks heard George's cry, he figured the Commies were carrying him down the slope. He went back in to look but couldn't see anyone so he came out to the trench and rolled a grenade that way, zinging fragments.

"Hearing it, George ran out the fighting hole, up the trench back toward the command bunker. Brooks saw the fleeting figure and cut loose with his M2 carbine.

"I was just starting to get up from the trench when the M2 started popping.

"Rosenbloom had fallen out of his bunk at the explosion and was coming out of the sleeping bunker when Brooks' carbine cut loose. He fell back in. Brooks worked his way to Dog Two. I and Rosenbloom came on as cautiously. When we met Brooks he told of the gasp and the sob, the fleeting figure and why he threw the grenades and fired his weapon.

"I whistled the phone to get the CP to tell them Brook's story. Both Dog and Charley Companies were put on 100 % alert. A squad worked down the forward slope. Nothing!

"It was dawn when the Top Kick caught sight of a GI next to the sand bags of the command bunker crawling out of a shelter half as if out of a cocoon. It wasn't a butterfly. It took a few days for me to get another replacement. This time I told the new guy all he needed to know about rats, never mind night crawlers."

Grandpa fell to quiet, his body in Union Township, his mind on the MLR.

Homer waited a second or so, then asked, "What happened to George?"

"George? He was in that cocoon. He took real well to the Regimental Motor Pool."

"That be my place in the Army," Homer said.

"In a cocoon?" Noah said

"Probably," Hezikiah said, looking at his hired man, "seeing he can't rebuild my motor to out run your's, Noah's."

"Right good yarn, Grandpa," Homer said, ignoring the jibes. "I worried on George."

"Me too," Hezikiah said. "I know it be hard to find good mechanics."

"As you be a walker on Union Township's roads and golf course, Grandpa," Noah said, "you must have got started on Korea's mountains as one of them USA infantrymen."

"Seems so!"

CHANGE

The joy of front porch sitting drained like water through a coffee strainer the while Grandpa watched the cattle trailers haul away Hezikiah's cows. Decades of dairy farming down the hill and across from the wetlands had come to an end.

Once, Grandpa's old farm house had been a part of a hundred and sixty acre farm with a herd of a prize cattle. The cattle were sold, the acres, but three, made a part of farmer Noah's grain farm. Years later he sold those acres to a golf course clan, and Grandpa's house sat across the road from a trailer club house and a half acre crushed stone parking lot. Front and back nines on either side of his house were filled with golfers hurrying golf carts in every direction.

A sharp increase in back road Union Township traffic followed. Hot roads became sausage skillets for crushed critters. Grandpa decked himself out in the brightest colors, a glowing and cautious road walker fearlessly facing car wash while waving as if all speeding by were first cousins come for a'kissing. Born and long time a townsman where traffic was second nature, he was long enough out in the country that the switch from tractors and pickups to cars of modern years was more than just noticeable. The kick-up from cars on the parking lot brought dust from the east as if his front porch, and its prime occupant, were subject to Vesuvius' moody soot.

When the politicians back in Washington cut income taxes, very little for Grandpa and Grandma, but a bank full for big money folks, construction rigs, vans and pickups found the back roads on their way to Lake Maxinkuckee. Little cottages that sold for big dollars were torn down, replaced by houses big as motels as out of place as buffalo fish on a Thanksgiving plate.

The quiet of Union Township's back roads, (not counting farm tractors, pickups, deer and pickup collisions, the daily mail delivery, weekly garbage truck or the bi-weekly recycle truck), had given away to big rigs, fancy cars, and golfers.

Hezikiah and Noah came on over to sit and gab on the front porch, surprising Grandpa by telling they both were retiring from farming. Hezikiah, yes. He'd sold his herd. But Noah? Hezikiah said he his Missus figured the time had come to sell, not having offspring attuned to twice a day milking when forty hour a week jobs could be had off the land. Noah was a widower with no kin inclined to farm. Though the farmers bodies were hard as granite from years of chores, hands wide as pie plates and hard as stone, health good, both were the upside of sixty-five. Their time to rest had come.

Hezikiah said, "Sold my Holsteins to that foreign fella who's putting in one of them big feeding operations. My tractor, self propelled hay mower, silage dump wagon, manure spreader, bulk tank, hoses, darn near everything out to the barn and in the sheds, sold. My land, barn, outbuildings and my house sold to a city fella."

"Then you're moving?" Grandpa said with regret in his words.

"In a manner of speaking," Hezikiah answered.

"And you, Noah?" Grandpa asked.

"Got me a deal with a share cropper."

"And you're moving?"

"In a manner of speaking," he said, a smile rippling his face like a lake wave did the sand.

Bothered by their play-fullness, Grandpa's grimace let them know, before he'd fetch the Yukon Jack, they better get on to the stories they'd come to tell.

"Well," Noah said, "me and Hezikiah are going to where it's warm of a winter. We got trailers side by side."

"On lots close to the ocean," Hezikiah said.

"Have you sold your farm, Noah?" Grandpa saked.

"Naw. Got me a sharecropper. After planting and harvest I'll come back to Union Township to check out the place. Kept me a room on the second floor."

"You've really got it worked out," Grandpa said. "What about Homer?"

"Here he comes now. Tell you when he comes up," Hezikiah said.

An '83 pickup had coughed to a stop. Hired man climbed out and hustled up to the porch and sat down.

"Good to see you Homer," Grandpa said.

"Big doings, right?" He said

"They were about to tell me."

"Homer's taking over Septic Slurp," Hezikiah said.

174

"We worked out a deal on the slurp truck. His boys be getting big enough to give him a hand."

"Are there enough septic tanks customers to make a living?" Grandpa wondered.

"If there ain't," Noah said, "Homer's going to be my sharecropper. Move into my place."

"He is? That's great!" Grandpa said. "Homer, you're going to be rich."

"Rich?" said Noah. "Not like that fella what bought Hezikiah's land."

"What's he going to do with it?" Grandpa asked.

"He ain't moving into the house," Hezikiah said. "That Real Estate fella told me the buyer's going build a big barn out in my alfalfa field and raise fancy horses."

"Rent the house?" Grandpa asked.

"Naw. Tear it down, the barn and sheds too."

"Why?"

"Don't know. Place is old, needed lots of work. I'm glad to miss that. Sure going to miss hopping across the road during hunting season."

"Season?" Noah said. "No matter the State said hunting duck, geese, deer had seasons, old Hezikiah here got his game."

"I was there long before they wrote that dadbern Law," he said.

"When I moved out here and went to walking the road," Grandpa said, "you should have warned me about hunters. That first time so many rounds were fired, it sounded like a Hatfields' and McCoys' feud. I hit the

175

ground and rolled into a ditch."

"Saw you slip down slope," Homer said. "When I got there, you were climbing out wetter than a fresh caught carp."

Smiles.

"I'll get the Yukon Jack."

Glasses filled, sips taken, they settled down for more palaver.

"Tell me about that foreigner who bought you cows. You said something about a big feeding operation."

"What I know about him was his money was good. About that there operation, it's big alright. Over three thousand five hundred cows on a hundred acres. Me and Homer had a hundred and forty head on more than a hundred acres, milking twice a day. What with milking, chores and farming, we be busy from dark to dark. Nowadays, family farming is fading away, changing to big operations backed by big business. To work that operation's herd, say one hired man every hundred or so cows, that's thirty or more on the payroll. That's big time, taking in account building sheds, buying equipment, trucking, feed, milking, manure removal."

"Lot of folks living out that way complaining about it," Noah said. "I took a look at what the Law required. There ain't no state or county law. I wrote the words down." Noah pulled out a sheet of paper and read: "'An application for a permit for an individual pollutant discharge elimination system.' Big words. The state's environmental people do an engineering review when they get the application. When that's complete, there's a hundred and eighty days for folks to look at it to give feedback. If state holds a public meeting, state answers only written questions sent in before. No public discussion. Can't stop it now, confined feeding of cows where it's at, and where it's zoned agriculture."

"If I remember rightly," Hezikiah said, "3,500 cows need about 1,300 gallons of water a day and drop 80,000 pounds of waste the same day. That big operation going need 4000 acres to spread manure."

"I can imagine some of the complaints," Grandpa said. "Right now, with the wind out of the northwest, I still get a whiff of cow scent, but I moved out to this old farm house knowing farms were operating, that it's zoned agricultural. Still, if Hezikiah had taken on his hundred acres another 3,000 cows, there would be more than a whiff out of the west. It could have been air pollution, ground water pollution, mosquitoes, dry wells and a stench to top the stench over to Mont Fulton."

"Mont Fulton?" Noah asked.

"The garbage dump over to the main highway. The smell from composing on its top is worse than the smell slurped from septic tanks. Mont Fulton is big time air pollution, and the toxic waste dump over to the east is leaking again. That's ground water pollution."

"Why do they bring it out to the country?" Hezikiah asked, "Most of that garbage and toxic stuff be made back in the cities and by their factories, right?"

"Right."

"Unfair," said Noah. "Those cities have acres of rust belts. They should dump their garbage and toxic wastes there. Who could tell one city stench from the others?"

"Hear tell they want to build an ethanol plant over east of Union Township to turn corn into whiskey," Homer said.

"Not whiskey like the old days," Noah said, "but ethanol. Good for grain farmer."

"Really? Grandpa said. "Here's Hezikiah closing a hundred and forty herd dairy farm, and up the road, big business opening one with over three thousand cows on fewer acres."

"Can't compete," Hezikiah said."I got a dollar a gallon in good times. Milking thousands of cows going cut into small farmers' income. Most, like me, will sell."

"And," said Grandpa. "Here's Homer taking over from Noah when the price of corn should go up."

"That's the times," Noah said. "Big business turning most farmers into hired men."

"And," Grandpa said. "I read an ethanol plant in Minnesota, a few years back, was closed by the Federal Environmental Protection Agency because of air pollution. Then I read politicians are making the EPA rewrite those rules, weakening the Clean Air Act because, in addition to the fifty ethanol plants already going, another fifty are on line, and the President wants ethanol to cut into oil imports."

"Whatever," Hezikiah said, "It be on the way, Big agriculture, the President, corn growers be behind it, and local folks want jobs close by."

"They are and local folks do," Grandpa said. "Big shots in politics and business will see to it, like they saw to the toxic waste dump coming to a rural township. The toxic dump is now bankrupt, closed and leaking chemicals. They brought the huge garbage dump to a farm county. Its grown to a mountain that stinks. Confined feeding and an Ethanol plant will come to our county and bring jobs, plus noxious odors and ground water contamination. Feeding those animals means manure lagoons bigger than public swimming pools and as smelly as politicians' reelection contributions. Times sure aren't changing."

PASSED AWAY

There were so many trucks lining the roads close to
and far away from those crunched into Holy Smoke
Church's parking lot, half the size of a basketball court,
Grandpa in a suit and tie, was on to thinking the deceased
was as popular as Union Township's Grand Champion Bull
over to the County Fair. It appeared likely, Grandpa
thought, a few in newly washed shirts and suits out of moth
balls came, not for the funeral, but for afterwards. The
word from Holy Smoke over Union Township was,
afterwards, there would be hot fried fish, home made pie
and cups of Lila's new fangled coffee like the stuff what
cost a day's pay in big towns' upscale coffee houses.
Grandpa admitted he didn't mind the eats, but his presence
was called for because he owed Delicta who'd helped him
fun Hezikiah with a rubber carp at the last church supper.

It weren't no big deal for Grandpa to walk the half
mile to church from where he parked his pickup. It gave
him time to notice the size of the gathering crowd
amounted to the size of the crowd at the last Holy Smoke
church supper. He figured it wasn't unusual for most
church members to join in the moaning, or for Hezikiah to
attend, for his hired man, Homer, was Delicta's boy. She, a
few months back, had gotten hitched to Pastor Reverend
Clem, himself. Or for Noah attending, seeing as he'd
escaped nuptials to Delicta and owed her eternal respect for
choosing Reverend Clem over him. But a high school bus

full of football players? Union Township nursing home's bus full of old geezers? Then again, Reverend Clem's part time job was driving the nursing home bus. The football players were regulars at fish fries. Besides, the Reverend preached for all Union Township folks to come to his church on bicycles, pickups or shoes, or without, come on his bus, for he had a bus for them.

A look given the old folks on the nursing home bus, Grandpa saw the Goldentones were dressed in their finery, a quartet plus three, helped off and carried upstairs, wheelchairs and all, by school bus footballers, none out of uniform, shirt and tie.

The organization of the final goodbye at Holy Smoke Church seemed top notch.

From the outside, the church looked country. Its sanctuary was elevated eight feet above ground by a field stone basement, the stones gathered from farmers' field and carted to the site, a basement dug and stone walls laid. It was done back in land grant days, the frame made from logs cut from nearby woods and horse pulled to the site, planks and siding cut, beams rounded, shingles sliced. White coats of paint covered the outside right up to the tent shaped steeple.

Inside the double door entry, hand made benches ran from the rear to the tabernacle, three steps up. Grandpa watched the footballers escort the Goldentones to the sanctuary, lifting them to places near the pulpit. Other football players, as pall bearers, brought the casket forward, standing along side as honor guards. Two lines of finery bedecked local folks were formed to pay last respects to the deceased, and having done so, took seats in the pews.

Although there was quiet chatting ongoing, the wailing of Homer cast a chill. He couldn't be consoled, even by Hezikiah, who, unlike himself, had an arm around his hired man, after managing to pry Homer's hands off the coffin.

But for the wailing, Grandpa wouldn't have recognized the dairy farmers in suits. Bib overalls were the twenty-four hour clothing of choice. Turning from the crying, Grandpa's view of the corpse caused a lot of blinking. No matter the skill of Aron, the undertaker, nothing could he do to change the beetle brow or the nose shaped like a ham hock. It must have taken all his skill to fit the full body into the casket, extra large.

Homer, noticing Grandpa at the casket, sobbed again. Hezikiah squeezed his hired man's hand. Hezikiah was most times a good man, but Homer was causing him mental profanity, and being as they were in church, he was quiet. The sorrowful hired hand was led to a pew to sit next to his Missus. Hezikiah and his Missus joined them, so too Noah, waitress Minerva, her black dress a tad tight, and café's Lila, draped under a black shawl.

Grandpa slipped between Noah and Minerva and whispered to the suit dressed grain farmer, "Homer sure is choked up!"

"He be worried," Noah whispered. "Some church folks be saying Reverend Clem done married Satan twice, the second wife doing him in."

"Folks think Delicta put Reverend Clem down?" Grandpa whispered, amazed.

"In a manner of speaking," Noah hissed. "Word is she sapped his strength in bed."

It took all Grandpa's inner control, limited as such was, to not split his sides. Fortunately, the Goldentones, like seven swallows, took that moment to break out in song:

'From every stormy wind that blows, from every swelling tide of woes,

There is a calm of sure retreat, 'Tis found beneath the mercy seat.'

A while back, only two of the Goldentones were in wheelchairs, now five. Though their bodies showed life was a chore living with physical lamentations, their spirits were upbeat.

Harmony over, didn't Pastor Round of Pleasant Hills Church and Minister Mont of Pond Wood Church lead a groaning and sniveling Delicta from out of a side door into the sanctuary. She was covered in Reverend Clem's clerical robe, and looked a worn out missionary. Reverends Round and Mont took bottoms to chairs, Delicta going up to the pulpit, standing behind it, the east and west of her protruding in those directions. She raised hands folded as if in prayer.

Chatting ceased, eyes boggled, Homer stopped sobbing. Grandpa could almost hear the congregations' surprise. The widow preaching? Not the ministers?

Delicta said, "Reverend Clem done told me this,

183

and seeing as how he passed before he could let you or the Reverends here in on it," she gave them a bow, "I'm going to do it for him." Her voice wasn't her usual nasal twang, but low as the bass in the Goldentones.

Arms high, she said, "An Angel appeared one night and told Reverend Clem there was a story to tell his flock, but Reverend Clem thought he'd been dreaming, so he paid it no mind. The next night the Angel returned and punched Reverend Clem upside his head," she led with her right, crossed with her left, 'for not paying attention the night before. He did when the Angel lifted him from bed to above where the moon circles the earth."

Her hands hovered above the pulpit.

"Said the Angel, 'Come see where the Just and Sinners go after taking leave of the earth.'" Delicta's index finger went up, then down. Beads of sweat formed on her creased forehead. "Up they went and the Angel said, 'Look down.'" She did. "Reverend Clem did and saw all the world and the people were as small as grains of sand on an ant's back."

She held out her right thumb, pointing to it as if infested, rubbing off imaginary sand.

"Then the Angel said, 'Now look at Union Township.' Clem did and saw Cecil, over to the nursing home, about to pass on. Tears was in Reverend Clem's eyes," and hers. "The Angel said, 'Cecil is a just man. His good deeds stand out in his hour of need.'"

"That's right!" hollered the Goldentones in tearful

harmony.

Delicta turned her head and nodded a blessing to the old folks, then rolled it back to her pew sitters and said,. "Reverend Clem saw holy Angels looking on Cecil. They took hold of his spirit when it passed, saying 'Come along to a place you've never known'."

Delicta pointed up. "The pretty voices of a hundred thousand Angels sang for Cecil, like these here Goldentones do for Reverend Clem."

"That's right," the Goldentones' Jo Ann sang.

"Then the Angel said to Reverend Clem, 'Look again down to Union Township and see Cory, a man who bought more liquor than groceries for his wife and kids, a man who scorned church going folks."

"He weren't much of a church goer," said Homer, the Hired Man, his Missus in accord.

Recognition supplied her boy, Delicta went right on, "Reverend Clem saw Angels go up to Cory, but back off."

"For sure," Homer said knowingly, having the mood of righteousness on him.

"Instead," Delicta said, "evil ones took hold of Cory when he passed and said, 'You have lost time for repentance.' A hundred thousand Angels yelled, 'Woe to you, Cory. Where is any good you have done?'"

Grandpa was impressed. Delicta was as g-o-o-o-o-d as Pastors Round and Mont.

"Then the evil ones said, 'Let Cory be cast into the outer darkness, a long way from Union Township.'"

"Amen!" echoed throughout.

Sadmor, the owner of the liquor store didn't amen.

Delicta bathed in the peoples' comeback. She said, "When the Angel again pointed, Reverend Clem looked and saw several Union Township folks who'd passed on. They were weeping and asking for mercy. The Angel said, 'When have you showed mercy to the very poor and sick in Union Township; or did good for your own children?'"

"Oh my!" exclaimed a lady in a bright sweater. "She's ain't talking only on Cory!"

Delicta didn't take time to deny it. Arms spread wing-like, she said, "Another Angel appeared with a list on paper of all the bad those Union Township folks had done, clear back to birth, and said, 'If any of you had changed your ways five years back, even one year ago, these records would have been thrown away, your slates clean. None of you changed your ways.'"

"I' a'going to," shouted old pinhead. He was shushed.

Delicta nodded as if she'd forgave him. "Then Reverend Clem's Angel said to him, 'If anyone in or outside Union Township does violence to someone in Union Township, the violent one shall be put to torment.'"

"Ain't never done that there violence to no one," Pinhead said, "just squirrels."

That brought a grimace to Delicta's puffed lips."Now you just calm down, Pinhead." She raised her hands as if signaling for quiet. "'Come,' the Angel said. He took Reverend Clem to the place of the Just, where there

186

was a door of gold, where entry was permitted only those who had lived a life of goodness. Reverend Clem saw a river flowing with milk and honey, the river's bank full of ripe fruit trees, grapevines, and everywhere an abundance of food for the worthy who'd done good for others."

"Oh heavenly days," a round woman, back pew, prayed.

"The Angel next took Reverend Clem to a river of wine, the place for all who have given hospitality to strangers. Then to a river full of relaxing warm water where Reverend Clem heard the singing of songs by those devoted to uplifting others."

A feeble man struggled to stand. "That warm water be for me," he said, his cane holding him up.

"Hope so, Bud. Better you sit," Delicta said. She again took off. "The Angel said, 'Come and I'll show you the place for the hardheaded located the other side of the ocean.' Reverend Clem was carried toward the setting of the sun, but there was no sunlight. He saw a river boiling with fire, some folks in the river up to their knees; some up to their mid-sections; some up to their lips, others up to their eyebrows. 'Who are they?' Reverend Clem asked. The Angel said, 'Those not yet numbered among the Just. Those up to their knees were the ones who left church services early; those up to their mid-sections slept during sermons; those up to their lips gossiped on church goers; those up to their eyebrows, nodded nicely to folks coming and going from services, but disliked them.'"

Heads turned to locate those in it up to their knees,

mid-section, lips or eyebrows

"At another river of fire there were pits. Reverend Clem asked, 'Who are those folks down there?' The Angel said, 'Those who skipped church of a Sunday. The pits have no bottoms for all yet to arrive.'"

Most women heads turned to their men.

"When Reverend Clem saw a man hooked like a fish being pulled by a hand without an arm or body, he said, 'Who is that in the fiery river?' The Angel said, 'A grocer who changed 'do not sell by dates' on food products.'"

Orville, the grocer, was in the 'skip church' crowd, so missed his moment of renown.

"'And the man being pushed by the evil ones into the fiery river?' Reverend Clem asked.

"'A money lender of pay day and title loans with killer pay back interest,' the Angel answered.

Flora, the good woman hitched to Walt, the record keeper, felt the heat of hot breaths.

Delicta let Flora fry awhile, then said, "When Reverend Clem asked why evil ones were carrying burning chains in their hands, the Angel said, 'to put around those who did he-ing and he-ing or she-ing and she-ing.'"

"That's right, like the good Book say at 1 Romans 26." Pastor Round, whose small facial features contrasted with puffed pop corn eyelashes, rose up as he approached the pulpit. Arms raised, hands tempted to point to more than one he-er or she-er, were restrained by Delicta. She escorted him back to his chair, and sat him down.

Back at the pulpit, she said, "When Reverend Clem saw men and women covered with ashes way down in a pit bubbling with pitch and sulphur, he asked, 'Who are they?' The Angel said, 'Unmarried men and women who burned with lust.'"

This time it was Pastor Mont, a tall, wide load man with a long face, who left his chair. He said, 'I told you so, Minerva. It's in the Good Book at 1 Corinthians 7'. Delicta spun him around, and reseated him.

Minerva welcomed the stares of football players. The more of them who chow down at Lila's café, more tips for a working woman.

Back again at the pulpit, spread either side of it, her face glowing, Delicta let go, "Over where there was a river of ice, Reverend Clem saw men and women whose feet were frozen in. The Angel said, 'Parents who didn't do right by their children.'"

Very few heads turned.

"Finally, before the Angel returned Reverend Clem home, he pointed to men and women standing near flowing fountains, but their tongues were dry as sandpaper. The Angel said, 'They are those who said bad words.'"

Every football player coughed as if all had come down with consumption.

Delicta let throats clear. "Back home, Reverend Clem was joyous, having seen the place where the Just go; joyless for those sent to fiery waters or deep pits. He told me all this, but passed on before he spoke it to you from the pulpit. I felt it my duty to preach it."

Many heads nodded agreement.

"Brothers, Sisters," Delicta said, "be called to the tree of knowledge as seen by Reverend Clem at the hands of an Angel. Hearken to his vision, become a new and abiding being."

Shouts of 'Amen' bounce off the rafters. There were tears and rustling among the congregation. Those who could stand, stood; those who couldn't, didn't; but all clapped hands.

Grandpa whispered to Noah, "Delicta's a hit."

"She surely is," Noah said. "Hope Holy Smoke's folks call her to preach."

"Worried if they don't, she'll recall your romantic slip of the tongue?"

"Yep! That be worse than being hooked like a fish pulled by a hand without an arm or body in the fiery river," Noah said.

The Goldentones closed the services harmoniously:

'Brief life is here our portion, brief sorrow, short-lived care,

The life that knows no ending, the tearless life is there.'

www.ingramcontent.com/pod-product-compliance
Lightning Source LLC
Chambersburg PA
CBHW071236130626
46556CB00003B/1036